Xanyic: Warrior Princess

The Origin Story

By: E. C. Robinson

I dedicate this book to my husband.

Honey, thank you for loving and supporting me throughout this adventure. You gave me the strength to write and now it can be shared with the world.

This one's for you, My King

Warning: *This book does not indicate that anyone has been abused. This book is purely fictional and is the result of a dream.*

How to Pronounce Certain Words

Xanyic: (Za-nique, like unique but not"

Mathyis: (exactly how it is spelled)

Zurnik: ('Zir' like sir and 'nik' like nick.)

Xan'Zuli: (Zan-zoo-lee)

Zul'ese: (Zoo-lease, like Chinese)

Myantu: (My-an-to)

Kyoto: (Key-o-toe)

Kromishkov: (exactly how it is spelled)

Prologue

Cries echo through the halls of the palace. "The baby's here! The baby's here!" a maid cries out. King Mathyis hurries into the bed chamber to see the Queen holding the beautiful bundle of joy. "It's a girl my love. Come say hello to your daughter." the queen says. Mathyis walks over and sits by her side. Taking the baby into his arms, he stares at the little beauty. "She is just as precious as can be Marie," he speaks. Observing the little one from head to toe, he focused on her eyes, which gleamed a bright golden yellow. Never had he ever seen such beautiful eyes. "We have to name her you know?" the Queen gestures. "This is true," he says. "But what should we name her? I want it to be perfect, just like her." Before the Queen can say a word, a knock sounds at the door. "The maids know not to interrupt us at this precious moment so who could that be?" Mathyis barks. Not the guards and especially not their assistant who made sure everyone dispersed. Suddenly, the doors to the balcony swing open with a gush of wind flowing in its wake. Three figures float into the room from the shadows. All three of them look dark and sinister, wearing long black cloaks that covered them from head to toe. Their hands are folded on their chest gracefully and you cannot see their faces. After coming to a stop, they turn to the King and Queen and say in unison," Fret not your majesties for we come in peace. We are the Seers three and we come with a prophecy." Their voices are deep and ominous. Marie shudders at the thought of how creepy they sound. The king draws his sword without hesitation. "Stay back!" he roars. "A prophecy is underway. For a princess is born on this very day. The sixteenth year a decision will be made. The ultimate battle of good and evil will be waged," says the Seers. Concern grows on the King and Queen as they continue. "Protect her and guide her for this is an important task. Not heeding this warning, will unveil the mask. A betrayal and darkness falling awaits. When the blood moon rises DEATH anticipates." Without warning, they shoot backwards out the same way they came, and the doors slam shut. Mathyis and Marie stared at each other nervously. Suddenly, the door to the bed chamber opens and a guard appears in a panic. "The palace is under attack sire!" he cries out. A loud bang causes the room to shake. Instantly, Mathyis is on high alert and hands the baby to Marie. "Get somewhere safe my love. I will handle this," he says to her. She nods and begins to stand with the help of her housekeepers who quickly found their way inside. Mathyis stands and faces the guard. "Secure the palace and guide the queen to the-" "Wait!" she yells and grabs his arm. "Let's name her Xanyic, after our home. Xan'Zuli is not only a great nation but the representation she gives will give the people hope." Mathyis kisses her and smiles, "Xanyic it is then." "Isn't this sweet?" A deep voice speaks in a low, evil manner. Mathyis flinches and he slowly turns around. His eyes go wide when he sees his best friend in the doorway stabbing his guard in the chest. "What the fuck are you doing Zurnik? Explain yourself!" "I have come for the child. Her powers will serve me well." He says. Mathyis growls at him and races forward grabbing him by his chest and shoving him onto the wall. "Over my dead body!" he yells. "How could you do this? I thought you were my friend." Zurnik chuckles. "We are friends Mathyis. You will always be my friend. But friendship is not enough for me. I. Want. More!" Zurnik pushes off the wall and they begin to fight. Mathyis punches him in the stomach. Zurnik throws him onto the floor, and they continue for the next few minutes. Marie cries in the corner and feels like she needs to do something, but she knows she must protect her baby. Then a thought pops into her head. She places the baby onto the bed and casts a protective spell on her. "You will be fine my darling.

Just wait here." She pushes off the bed and grabs one of the collective swords her husband keeps in the corner. "Stay away from my husband you monster." She demands. The sword begins to glow brightly, and she begins to lunge forward. Another loud boom erupts throughout the palace, and everyone falls on the floor. The floor cracks around the bed and Marie begins to panic. "Mathyis, the baby!" she yells. Everyone looks at the bed and freezes. Next thing they know, they see Xanyic floating in mid-air with a glowing light shining around her. She is crying but no one can get to her. And then, she vanishes. "No!"

Tragic right? Well, you just wait. Our story is just beginning.

Chapter 1

I stare into the mirror of my bedroom. Sporting the black grunge look of my favorite rock band, black ripped jeans, and platform boots I sighed in utter boredom. "This is as good as its going to get I suppose," I say. Not even bothering to comb my long thick hair, I throw on my coat and grab my book bag. "Sarah! Get your ass down here now!" my uncle yells from downstairs. "Ugh!" I grunt, throwing my head back. "I'm coming!" Rolling my eyes, I fly out of my room door and descend the stairs. As I reach the bottom step, I am greeted with the smell of heavy smoke and alcohol. "What the hell took you so long girl? You better not be late for school again or it's the attic for you this weekend." My Uncle Tommy stares at me while pulling a puff of his cigarette. It's not even eight o'clock in the morning yet and he is already drunk. You can tell he has been up all night from the dark circles under his eyes and the fact that he is still wearing the ketchup-stained shirt and jeans from the night before. Man, he looked a mess. He also reeks like he hasn't showered in a few months, but I know not to tell him that. Doing so will cause more issues than I can handle right now, and I try to avoid the punishment of the attic as much as possible. I clear my throat and ask, "Um….is Aunt Carol driving me to school today?" As if on cue, she cuts around the corner grunting. "And why in the hell would I do that? You got two damn legs you can walk to school! I am not wasting my gas or time with you." "But its three blocks away to get to school and its pouring outside." I utter in protest. "Don't you sass your aunt little girl!" my uncle snaps. He raises his hand like he is about to smack me, and I flinch. I know what you're thinking, how can your own family treat you so poorly, especially on your birthday. Yes, it's my sixteenth birthday today and no one seems to care. Well, according to my parents, my aunt and uncle are just simply no good. And no one would think that it was a smart idea for me to live with them but unfortunately, my parents died when I was ten in a car accident while I was sleeping over at a friend's. I used to live in North Carolina with them before I had to move in with my aunt and uncle who now live in Florida. They just couldn't bear to see their only niece be passed around in the system and be given to cruel and terrible people. So, they felt it was their Christian duty to take responsibility for me because they are the only family I have left. Yeah right! How ironic is that? They only did it for the money and they could care less about me. My uncle starts chuckling at me. Maybe because I gave him the response he was looking for with that action or maybe because he just sees me as this weak little toy that he can torture as much as he wants. I scurry past them and fly out the door. "Oh, and Sarah, you better be home on time today, we want our dinner at seven tonight and then we are heading out so if your late, that's your ass!" My aunt hollers after me. I dash down the street until I am no longer in view of my house. When I know I am in the clear, I pull out the umbrella from my bookbag, thanking God that I remembered I had it stored in there for moments like this. Pulling it out, I try to hurry along before I miss first period.

"Chica! It's about time you got here. What took you so long? You almost missed the bell." I walked into my first class to find my friends, Candace, and Rachel. Candace or Candy for short looks at me with her usual sassy demeanor. Candy is an African American with long brown wavy hair, smooth dark skin, blue eyes that can stop traffic and has a lot of attitude. Not the bad kind of attitude but the intimidating kind that leaves people feeling like you're weird and don't want to be around you. She is around my height, a measly five foot five and she will not hesitate to speak her mind. A lot of people would label her ghetto, but I believe she has the kindest soul ever. Rachel is Caucasian with thick, curly, bright red hair, innocent brown eyes, and a very gracious smile, flashing perfect white teeth. She is beyond the sweetest southern bell to ever walk this earth. Rachel is shorter than both of us but not by much. She is four foot nine but the way she constantly wears heels to go with her classy attire, you would think she is five foot one. What they see in me I will never understand but I am glad to call them friends. "Yes, we were worried that you wouldn't be coming in today." Rachel says, taking my hand. I give a small smile and sit at my desk in between them. "Um hello? Earth to Sarah." Candy says waving her hand frantically in my face. "Sorry, sorry." I speak lowly. "I was struggling to get out of the house. I didn't even get the chance to eat. I had to run to make it here on time." "Ya aunt and uncle giving you a hard time again ain't they?" Candy asks angrily. "Girl just say the word and I'll give both they asses a piece of my mind. You know I ain't scared of either one of them and best believe honey, if they try me, I will not hesitate to cut them." Rachel looks at Candy with a disappointing look. "Now Candy you know that is no way to settle matters with people. If you want to get the most progress out of a situation, then you must be able to sit down like adults and iron out the problem. I'm sure they would be willing to hear you out." We both look at her like you can't be serious. "Rach are you thick in the head? You know damn well this ain't no fairytale and they ain't gon' listen." Candy protests. I nod in agreement. "We all know my aunt and uncle to be cruel and harsh so there is no way talking to them will help the situation." I say to her. "Alright class, settle down." Mr. Santiago announces. "Everyone find their seats." I sigh with relief that this conversation is over and slump in my chair. Candy leans over and whispers, "I hope you know this ain't over and we will finish this conversation later miss thang." I roll my eyes at her and smile. For the next few hours, I quietly write in my notebook each lesson the teachers give awaiting lunch so I can relax. The day goes by in a blur as two of my classes have already passed me by and lunch finally comes around. I always have mixed feelings about lunch. I like it because I can sit with my friends for half an hour and enjoy their company. I despise it because the Popular's do not hesitate to pull a fast one on me and somehow end up embarrassing me. I grab my lunch and quickly make my way to the back of the cafeteria so that I cannot be seen by them. Candy and Rachel find me with my head down and hurry over to me. "Girl if you don't hold your head up. We will not have our best friend sulking and trying to hide on her birthday." Candy says confidently. "Yeah, Sarah Candy is right. It's your birthday. You shouldn't be hiding like this." Rachel says. I look at both of them and put my head back down. "Y'all know why I do this." I say to them lowly. "I am not in the mood to deal with Tiffany and the torture squad. I am not feeling too good, and I want to get through this day without any issues." Before I know it, here comes Tiffany. Tiffany, like every other story, is the most popular girl in school. She is captain of the cheer team, she was prom queen, head of the honor society, and blah blah blah. To me, she is just another mean girl in the sea of mean girls who somehow in some way all want to shoot arrows at me. "Oh my gosh, Sarah, I totally heard it was your birthday today. Is it true?" Tiffany asks smiling. *She seems a little too giddy to talk to me,* I think to myself. "Fuck off fake ass! We don't want you over here." Candy snaps. Tiffany just smiles and takes a seat. Her minions stand behind her, one holding her purse and phone and the other holding a present in her hand. "Come on guys, we come in peace." She says innocently. She snaps her fingers, and her minion Carolyn hands her the present. She places it on the table and slides it to me.

"Happy birthday Sarah. Sixteen is a big number and I wanted you to feel special on your day." I stared at her intensely, my suspicion of her growing by the second. "This present looks questionable to me." Rachel says to her. "If you don't want it, then you don't have to have it and I can return it." She snaps. I stare at the present a while longer before she stands up. "I'll let you think it over huh? If you do not want it, then you can leave it on the table, and I will take it back to the store." Tiffany flashes a smile and retreats to her usual table with her friends. "I don't trust that heffa to save my life honey." Candy says. "I would just leave it right there or better yet, throw the shit back in her face and tell her to fuck off big time." "Yeah Sarah. We all know that Tiffany and her goonies are always up to no good." I look at both of them. *I really don't want to deal with Tiffany's mess, and I know my friends know it to. Do I really want to indulge in their childish games knowing I am not in the mood nor am I feeling well?* I think to myself. *I do not know the feeling that is producing in my body but it's unsettling. I feel like a wave of energy is building within me or maybe I am just feeling overly confident on the inside but what I do know is that I have never felt this way before. It came on so suddenly and I'm not sure what to do about it. I mean yeah, I am starting to feel different, but in what way?* "Sarah? Sarah?" I blink to find my friends still staring at me. "I'm sorry guys. Was I staring off again?" I ask shyly. "Girl, are you alright? You're doing way more than just staring off. It's like you're in space or something because we can't get a word out of you." Candy places her arm on my shoulder, looking concerned. "Look Sarah, you know we are here for you. Just talk to us." Rachel says. "Guys I"- Suddenly the present jumps. We all freeze and stare at it. "What the hell?" I say confused. It jumps again. Then a third time. "Tiffany what bullshit are you trying to pull now?!" Candy yells from across the room. I look at them to see them laughing at us. The entire cafeteria is staring at us trying to figure out what is going on. Then the box starts to jump rapidly. Panic swells within me and I place both hands on my chest. "Sarah get away from that thing!" Candy yells. But before I could move an inch, the box exploded sending chunks of food, and sticky, brown liquid in my direction. I become mortified. Screaming at the top of my lungs the entire cafeteria breaks out in a roaring laughter. I look around to see pointed fingers and endless laughter at me. I am beyond pissed off at Tiffany. *How could she be so cruel to someone who does not even bother her?* I think. The anger I feel towards her starts growing and growing. I have had enough. I am sick of the teasing and the joking around and the bullying that I march over to where she is. *What is happening to me?* I think. *I cannot control myself.* A rage in me that I have never felt before arises to the surface with the intent of punishing her for everything she has ever done to me. I stand before her with my fist clenched ready to attack. "You're such a freak Jones!" she laughs. My rage is at its peak. I can't keep it in any longer. I shoved the table out of the way and grabbed her by her blouse. A look of shock flashes over her face and the room gets quiet. "You listen to me bitch!" I snap loudly. I punched her in the face so hard, she fell out of her chair. "I am so sick of these stupid ass games you play with me." I punched her again. "You. Will. Pay!!!" I began punching her at a rapid pace. I can't seem to stop myself. She needs to pay. I punched her a final time and she fell to the floor. The rage I feel instantly fades away and I shake my head in confusion. *What happened to me?* I think to myself. *I feel weak.* I place my hand on my head and shake my head again. I feel so weak that I stumble backwards, and my friends catch me. "Are you alright honey?" Rachel asks. "I don't know." I say. I look up in a haze to see the table is across the room, halfway outside the cafeteria wall and Tiffany's blood is splattered everywhere. My eyes go wide in astonishment. "Did I do that?" I ask. "Girl, you beat that bitch's ass!" Candy says proudly. "Eh, but she deserved it." Next thing we know, the principal, Mr. Kyoto comes over with security and the nurse. "Sarah Jones? I think you need to come with me." He speaks. The look of disappointment flashing across his face. He folds his arms waiting for me to rise. Security comes along and helps me stand. I groan, "I'm in big trouble."

Chapter 2

I sit in the principal's office waiting for my aunt and uncle to arrive. The principal sits at his desk, hands folded by his chest and just stares at me. He looks so angry that I am afraid to utter a word. Shoot I'm scared to even cough. "Miss Jones, I don't understand why this incident occurred" he says. "I don't believe you understand how much trouble you are in. As soon as your family arrives, I will discuss it further with them." As if on cue, my aunt and uncle entered the room. "Oh, my goodness! Sarah are you alright?" my aunt asks, sounding concerned. "What is this I hear about you being in trouble?" I shake my head not responding. I look at my uncle and he is giving me the most uncomfortable look he has ever given. He looks as though he is just upset and worried, but in his eyes, I can see nothing but a lifetime of misery in my future. "Mr. and Mrs. Edwards please have a seat." Mr. Kyoto ushers them to sit in the chairs. They sit quietly as the principal continues. "Now I know this is inconvenient for you all so I will not take up too much of your time. Sarah"- "Let me stop you there Mr. Kyto" my aunt interrupts. "It's Mr. Kyoto, ma'am." He corrects. "Well, that is what I said isn't it?" she asks confusingly. She looks at my uncle then back at Mr. Kyoto. "Anyway, Sarah is a good girl, and this is highly irregular of her to be acting out this way. Now she tells us she has been bullied and it seems she finally snapped her cap. So, I believe that this was an act of self-defense." I look at my aunt in astonishment. *Did she really just come to my defense like that? What's the trick? Maybe the sky is falling or something. I know my aunt and she does not give two shits about me so why is she acting this way?* I paused and then it dawned on me. *She wouldn't have an automatic change of heart. This must be for show. To show that she is a concerned aunt.* I roll my eyes at the thought. "That may be so and yes

I agree she is an excellent student, but an assault of this magnitude can only mean expulsion." Mr. Kyoto said. "What?!" I rise in protest. "You cannot be serious?" I start stammering my words. "I, I, I get straight A's, I stay out of trouble, I, I help with any kind of volunteer work. Mr. Kyoto I am one of your best students in this school!" Tears start to fill up in my eyes. "Miss Jones, please calm down." Mr. Kyoto says. "I know of your accomplishments, but I cannot excuse the fact that you destroyed school property and put a student in the hospital. I was fortunate enough to make sure Miss. Kromishkov's parents did not press charges." "It's not like I meant to, sir." I explained the situation with tears rolling down my face. "She came over to my table, carrying a gift. She said it was for my birthday which is today, but it turned out to be a food bomb. I mean look at my appearance." I raise my hands in a gesture of my body. "You know as well as I that I did not arrive here like this. She really has been bullying me ever since I arrived at this school, and no one has done anything to get her to stop. At least I stood up for myself instead of thinking suicidal." Mr. Kyoto looks at me with anger. "Would you like a dead body on this school's head?!" I yell. "That's enough Miss Jones!" He snaps. "Sit down, now!" My uncle grabs me by the back of my shirt and shoves me into the chair. He whispers in my ear, "Shut the fuck up or I'll knock out all of your teeth." I sit back and fold my arms feeling defeated. My uncle sits up and goes to ask, "Are you sure she cannot just get suspension for an extended time or some community service? You know, something that does not get her thrown out of school." Mr. Kyoto shakes his head. "Unfortunately, no. I cannot allow violence in my school, and I certainly do not want to start a panic with the other students or their parents because they are afraid of Miss. Jones. I'm sorry." My uncle nods his head and rises to shake Mr. Kyoto's hand. "We understand sir. Thank you for your time." We all stand and head towards the door when Mr. Kyoto calls after me. "Sarah! For what it's worth, I know you are a great person with incredible intelligence. Do not let others dictate your actions. Your future is bright, and we do not want something like this to keep you from whatever dream you seek." I nod my head, unable to stop the tears from flowing. "Take care of yourself, okay?" I nod again. He hugs me and I walk out of the school with my aunt and uncle. Getting close to the car I hear my name being called. I turn around to see Candy and Rachel running down behind me. "Girl, we heard what happened. Are you good?" Candy asks out of breath. "No. I'm being kicked out of school." I sob. "And who knows what's in store for me when I get home. Look at their faces." I whisper. They both look up over my shoulder at my aunt and uncle then back at me. "Well honey just know that we will always be there for you, okay? And when you get away from the hell hounds make sure you hit a sista up." Candy says and then hugs me. Rachel looks at me with tears starting to form in her eyes. "We are sure gonna miss you." She hugs me. "Please don't forget to call us, okay? And maybe if you can, we can still hang out after school." I laugh. "Yeah, we can definitely do that." They waved goodbye to me as I got in the car, and I watched as my two best friends fade from my view.

The car ride home was scary quiet. No one said a word to me or to each other. I just knew they were going to kill me. *Maybe they were plotting which death tools to use to decapitate my body.* I think to myself. *One cuts me up and the other digs a hole to bury me in.* As soon as I thought about it, I shoved the thought out of my head. We arrive at the house, and I am terrified of getting out of the car. "Get out you piece of shit." My uncle opens my door and grabs me by the arm. He slaps me across the face. "Look at the mess you got us in now!" He slaps me again. "You are in for a world wind of hurt'n little girl." He takes his belt off and starts slashing my back with it. I take off running towards the house and he follows in my wake. My aunt leans against the car and pulls out her cigarettes. "Tommy, baby don't hurt her too much. She may deserve the ass whooping but we can't kill her." my aunt shouts while lighting a cigarette. She takes a puff and slowly starts walking towards the house laughing sinisterly. I ran around the house to try to at least tire my uncle out, but he charged at me like a bull. He sees nothing but red and I'm the red cloth he must strike down. I ran into the kitchen; he struck my arm. The living room, he strikes again at my ankles. When I reach upstairs and almost to my room, he strikes me again with the belt, but this time it smacks me across my face. The pain is excruciating, and it starts to blur my vision. I struggle to focus but I don't want to give up. I must get away from him. I look behind me to see how far he is away from me. I turned back around and immediately ran into the side of the doorway. I hit the wall so hard I passed out cold.

I awake to the feeling of pain emanating all over my body. *I feel like shit.* I think to myself. I sit up to look around and notice that I am in the attic, and it is raining outside. My head is thumping loudly, and my face feels swollen. I look over to the mirror in the corner and see that my cheek is indeed swollen, an awful black and blue color. "Oh God" I whisper. "I look terrible." I grab hold of a box and try to push myself up, but the pain is too painful to move. I slump back down onto the floor and put my hands over my face and begin to cry. I start to relive the events of today and cry even harder. "How could my life come down to this point?" I ask myself. "I don't understand it. How could one person have such bad luck and be condemned to such a terrible fate?" I curl up into a ball and continue to cry until I cannot cry anymore. When I was finally able to stop crying, I scooted to the only window in the attic and propped myself against the wall to listen to the rain. It sounded so peaceful. I actually enjoy the sound of rain, especially thunderstorms. I closed my eyes and inhaled deeply for the first time today. I stare outside into the backyard and say, "I just wish my luck would change. No one deserves this kind of torture." I look up at the stars and whisper a silent prayer. I continue to look out of the window when I see a small glowing light in the corner of my eye. I look at the direction it is coming from when I see a small chest on the opposite side of the room. I make my way to the light, feeling strangely calm and warm. You would think I would be afraid of it, but I'm not. I reach the mysterious chest and place my hand on it to grab it. As soon as I do, the light goes away. My hands slowly grab the box and place it on my lap. I lift it to see if it's locked and find that it is not. Lifting it all the way open, I scroll through the contents to find old pictures of my parents and I when I was younger. I glance at each picture, remembering each moment of our adventures. "God, I miss you guys so much." I whimper. I know it's been six years since they past, but I could never come to terms with their death. They were my parents after all. They loved and nurtured me my whole life. Supported me when I wanted to pursue a goal, they were there for me through my heartbreak, and so many more precious moments. My chest starts to feel heavy, and my heart starts hurting. I cannot contain my tears as I continue to stare at their faces. "Mom, dad?" I whisper. "I miss you guys so much. I am sorry I let you guys down. I hope you can forgive me." I clutch the photos and hold them to my chest. After holding it for a few long moments, I pull them away and continue to dig through the chest. Little trinkets my mother kept, badges from my father's boy scout troop, a torn piece of cloth, and some birthday cards. "Hmm......I guess that's all they decided to leave." I say. I start to put the items back into the chest when a letter falls on the floor next to me. I look at it and it has my name on it. I put the chest in between my legs and grabbed the letter. I open it and see the beautiful cursive handwriting. I ran my fingers over it and realized that it was my mother's handwriting. *Why did she write me a letter?* I think. Pushing the questions out of my head, I read the letter.

Dear Sarah,

If you are reading this, then that means that your father and I have passed away. I am writing you this letter to finally tell you the truth about yourself. But before I get into that, I need you to know that your father and I love you very much and nothing on this earth or the next will ever change that. With that being said, we both wanted you to know that you are adopted and that we are not your real parents.

I froze. I stared at the parchment in disbelief. Adopted. The word echoes in my head. "This cannot be happening." I whimper. Tears swell up in my eyes and I cannot contain them. They trickle down my face, slowly at first, then a waterfall of tears spur out of me. "How can I be adopted?" I say through my sobs. I try to pull myself together and continue to read the letter.

Please do not hate us. We wanted to tell you when you were older but as you can see, we never got the chance to. We found you in an alley around the corner from our house. It was around the area where the old mechanic shop was located. There was no name, no letter or anything for us to identify you. We went to the police to see if we could find your parents, but no one claimed you. We couldn't let you go once we had you, so we adopted you ourselves. All we have that is originally yours is the emerald green silk blanket that you were wrapped in. The blanket has a crest on it, and I believe it is your family's crest. Now my little dove, you know the truth. We want you to be happy. So, if being happy means coming up with a plan to find your real parents which I already know that you are, then you go and be happy. You can start by going back to the shop and looking for clues. It's a risk but I know you can figure it out. Good luck to you, my little one, and just know that your father and I will always be with you, okay?

Love always,

Mom

P.S. Please pack plenty of clothes, be mindful of strangers, and do not do anything impulsive. Gives us peace of mind in the afterlife.

I chuckle at my mom's final words. "Still being a mother even after you have passed." I say. I fold the letter back up and pull out the silk blanket. I notice that it's torn down the middle which explains the other half I tossed on the floor next to me. I pick the other half up off the floor and fold them both together. I came across the crest that my mother mentioned and tried to make sense of it. I see two golden birds standing opposite from each other looking away from each other. The birds look spectacular, but I frown at the thought that this species is unrecognizable.

Pushing the thought aside, I continue to stare at it. Both birds have one foot clutching onto what looks like a very beautifully woven vine that makes up the entire crest. Finally, the other foot clutches a white ribbon that has what looks like a family motto. The words, however, are in a language that I cannot understand. "But if I find my family," I say with a sly grin. "They will be able to tell me." So, gather everything, place it back in the chest, and begin planning my escape.

Chapter 3

I awake to the sound of birds chirping and the sun beaming on my face. I jerk myself forward to avoid the light being that it is too bright for my eyes. I look around and see that I am still in the attic. I groan at the thought. Sitting up and propping myself up on the wall, I rethink my plans to escape. I stayed up well past midnight to make sure that my plan would work. It would be a risky one, but I know that I must get out of this house as soon as possible. Nothing was holding me back from leaving. Reading that letter from my mom gave me the courage to take charge of my life. No more being pushed around, no more being abused, just nothing but pure freedom. It was so close that I could just feel it throughout my entire body, and I knew I had to grab hold of it. The only way to really achieve it was to leave. I grab the small chest and push myself to my feet. The pain that was emanating from my body the day before had calmed down tremendously. I look in the mirror and notice that my swollen cheek has gone down as well. It was, however, still an ugly black but at least I was healing. I tip toe my way to the door and turn the knob to see if it was locked. It was. "Way to keep me in here Unc." I whisper. I look around the room at my surroundings. I see my grandmother's old sewing kit and remember that she keeps supplies in there for when she sews. I made my way to it and started digging through the kit box. I stumble across a few Bobbie pins and begin to thank the heavens that she kept them there. I take the pins back to the door and bend them to form what could pass as a key. "I gotta thank Candy for showing me how to do this." I say. Back when I was younger and first meeting Candy, we used to get into lots of trouble. She even showed me how to pick locks on old doors. "Ya never know when you need to sneak your way to freedom honey." I remember her telling me back then. Chuckling at her words, I bend down and try to pick the lock. After trying a few times, the door lock clicks. I turn the knob and smile when it slowly opens with a low creak. I stick my head outside the door and listen to see if my aunt and uncle are awake. Hearing them last night, it was clear that they were beyond drunk and could possibly still be asleep. I grab the chest and tip toe my way down the steps, onto the second floor. I peek around the corner, and they are nowhere in sight. I take a deep breath and slowly make my way to my room. It's clear that they are still asleep and a good thing to. If I were to be caught, I would be getting it for sure. Pushing the thoughts away, I continue my pursuit. I get a few steps away from my door and I hear a creak in the floor. I freeze. "Lord, please don't let them hear that and wake up." I whisper. No one shows up. I breathed a small sigh and finally reached my door. I slowly open it and close it right behind me. I lean against the door and exhale deeply. *I completed step one. Thank God. Halfway done. Father please be with me.* I think to myself. I sit the chest down on my dresser by the door and grab my bookbag that was left on my bed. I frown as I stare at it. *I'll no longer be in school with my friends.* I think to myself. *I will miss them. I need to be sure to call them when I get the chance.* I shake my head to push the thoughts away. "I gotta stay focused. They will be waking up soon." I empty my bag and grab some clothes and other necessities and shove them all in there. Placing the small chest at the top, I zip up the bag and wipe my forehead. I look around the room and nod my head as a final goodbye. I grabbed my bookbag, threw it on my shoulders and made my way to the door. *Now I just gotta get past their room and out the door without making any noise.* I think to myself. I crack open my door and look to see if anyone is out in the hall. When I see no one, I quickly walk out of the room and close the door behind me. I turn around and tip toed once again to the stairs and slowly walk down them. I make it downstairs without being noticed and make my way to the kitchen. I look around and no one is down here. The place is empty. Looking outside I see that their car is parked outside. I shrugged. I reach the back door and stop. "This is too easy." I say to myself. "Going somewhere?" a low voice says behind me. I freeze. *Damn it!* I think to myself. *I knew it was too good to be true.* I turn around to see my uncle standing in the kitchen doorway. His hands are folded close to his chest, and he looks pissed. The sight of him sends chills down my back but I know that I have to stand up to him if I want to get out of here. "I said, going somewhere?" he growls. I close my eyes, take a deep breath, and stand up straight. "I'm leaving." I say somewhat proudly. "Oh really?" he says. "And where do you think you're going you little runt?" He slowly walks towards me. I tried to back up, but the door had me stuck in place. *You can do this Sarah.* I chant. I raise my head as he approaches me. We are now standing face to face. He gives me a creepy grin and it makes my stomach turn in knots. "I own you bitch and the only thing you are going to do is march back up those stairs and get back in that attic." He snaps. "You're not about to fuck up my money. The state pays us well for you and I don't have to work anymore as long as you are here." He forcefully grabs my arm. I wince at the pain. "Now you're gonna be punished even more since you left the attic. Maybe I need to buy a steel cage to keep you in line." He smirks. I shoved my hand away from his grip. "No!" I yell. "No more punishments, no more abuse, no more torture. I know the truth asshole. You're not my real uncle, she's not my real aunt and my parents are not my real parents." The confidence I feel as I am saying this is making all the weight evaporate from my shoulders. "I am leaving to find my real folks and you cannot stop me. No one can, you hear me?" That did it. He back hands me right across the face and I fall to the floor. I look at him as he approaches me, the anger emanates from his whole body. He is out for blood. "You little bitch!" he yells. He punches my shoulder. "You're not going anywhere!" He punches again and it lands on my chest. "Your mine!" He punches me again and it hits my face. I am starting to see stars at this point. *Lord, please make it stop.* I pray to myself. Then as if my prayers were answered, a sudden power overtakes me, and I grab his hand. "Get. Off. Of. Me!" I yell in pieces. I shove him off me and rise to my feet. This feeling is powerful and a burst of confidence spreads over me. I throw a punch and it lands in his face. He stumbles backwards into the living room and falls on the floor. I ran to him fast as lightening and kicked him in the stomach. He yells in pain with the pressure of the blow. At this point, he is rolling on the floor trying to get back to his feet. I grab him by the shirt and pull him close to my face. "You do not own me." I grit under my teeth. I punched him in the face and pulled him back to me. "I am leaving, and I am never coming back." I punch him again and he falls to the floor, the floor itself caving in with the power of the blow. I became beyond shocked at myself. I look at his body, folded up in a ball with cracks and half broken pieces of wood surrounding him. *Did I seriously punch him through the floor?* I ask myself. I hear the floor creek and I look up to see my aunt staring at me from the bottom of the steps. "I know the truth Aunt Carol. All of it. The adoption, how my parents found me, all of it." I say to her straightening myself up. "I am leaving, and I am not coming back." She just stands there and nods her head. You can look at her face and see how terrified she is. *Maybe she is wondering if I killed him or not.* "Don't worry. He is not dead." I say softly. "I just have to go. And don't come find me. This is my choice and I deserve to make this choice. You both ruined me enough so surely you can let me have this." She shakes her head and waves her hands frantically. "No, no you are right. Go and live your life. You don't have to worry about us anymore. Just please leave." She really is scared. Probably worried that I will hurt her too. I calmly nod my head and make my way to the kitchen. I looked in the cookie jar and took the emergency cash that I know is mine that they hid from me and put it in my book bag. I look back at her and she is still in the same place, staring at me. I nod and walk out the door to freedom.

Chapter 4

I walk down the street from the house, elated to finally be away from that hell hole. I look around and stumble across the park. It's Saturday, so the park is flooded with children running, jumping, and playing. I breathed in deeply and exhaled, not knowing that I was holding my breath. It feels good to be able to finally breathe. I smile at the thought. Taking another breath, I start walking down the road again. I reach the corner and look around. "I have to find my way to North Carolina if I am going to find my parents." I say aloud. I turned the corner and saw the gas station. I walk to it thinking, *"Maybe they have a map, or I can get directions to the bus station."* Picking up my paste, I grab a scarf from my bag, cover my face with it, and make my way inside the store. "Welcome to the Handy Mart." The cashier says dully. You could tell that she was bored and didn't care about her job. I walk up to her and say, "Hi. Do you by chance sell maps?" She looks up at me from filing her nails. "What?" she says with attitude. "I said, do you sell maps here or can I get directions to the bus station." She rolls her eyes at me and goes back to filing her nails. "Why would we sell maps in a gas station? Those things are old as fuck." She says dryly. I shake my head at her words. "Guess I'm not going to be getting any help here." I say lowly. I turned around and found an elderly lady behind me smiling. "Hello my dear." She says happily. I smile at her, "Hello ma'am." "I'm sorry to bother you sweetie but I couldn't help but overhear your question." Her smile gets wider as I look at her. "You don't need a map to get to the bus station. It's about five or six blocks down the road. That way." She points. I look down the road and back at her. "Oh, thank you ma'am." I say with excitement. "Oh, it's no problem, dear." She says back. I purchased some snacks and set my sights on the road to the bus station.

I barely make it to the station, and I see a long line of people boarding the bus. I look at everyone boarding, and I begin to get nervous. I ran to the ticket booth and trip over my own two feet. I jump back up and brush myself off. "Sorry." I say nervously as I look at the clerk. He looks at me with concern. "Uh, can I help you little lady?" he asks. I nod my head. "Yes, I would like a ticket to Charlotte, North Carolina please." He stares at me, not sure if I'm serious or not. By my appearance alone, I look like I am trying to run away. He sighs, "Go home kid. I am not losing my job just because you want to run away from home." I shake my head. "I'm afraid I cannot do that." I say maturely. He looked at me, surprised at my words. "Excuse me?' he says. I lean on the counter. "Here's the thing sir." I begin. "I am not running away, and frankly what I am doing is not your concern. Now it is of grave importance that I make it to my destination on time. So, are you going to do your job and issue me a ticket, or do we need to get your supervisor here?" I know that I am pushing it a bit by trying the man, but I need to get this ticket and leave this place as soon as possible. Plus, now is not the time to play the hero. I am pressed for time. He shakes his head and smirks. "Fine. Will it be one way or round trip?" I smiled at him with relief. "One way, please." He goes to his computer and types in the destination. After a few minutes he says, "Okay if you want the quickest route, it will be two hundred fifty-five dollars and ninety-eight cents." I nod my head as I reach into my book bag for my money. As I count the correct amount, he says, "If you want to catch that bus then you must hurry. It leaves in five minutes." I handed him the money and grabbed the ticket. "Thanks." I say just before running out to the bus. I look around for the correct bus and see that it is about to pull off. I wave my hands and dart my way towards it. "Wait! Don't forget about me!" I yell. The bus does not stop, and I begin to worry that I will miss it. Just when I think all hope is lost, my feet pick up the pace. I zoom across the field in a flash, appalled that I was able to do so. As I got closer to the bus, I try to slow down but I couldn't. I slam into the bus, and it comes to a quick stop. The door opens up and the driver comes to my side. "Are you crazy?! You could have hurt yourself you know?" I place my hand on my head and groan. "I'm sorry. I didn't want to miss the bus." He shakes his head and helps me to my feet. "Your insane for doing that. But I am glad you are not hurt." I smile at him as he escorts me onto the bus and into a seat in the back. "Now if there are no other interruptions, I would like to continue on my route. Let's just hope this stunt of yours doesn't delay anything." I hold my head down, feeling bad. "Sorry again." He walks to the front of the bus and begins to drive. I slouch in my chair, feeling relieved I made it. I exhaled slowly, trying to register everything that happened today. *I still can't believe that I beat Uncle Tommy up and broke the floor in the process.* I think to myself. *And how was I able to push the table through the cafeteria wall? Was I ever this strong before? Or fast? I don't remember any of this.* I look out the window and watch as different buildings pass by as we make our way to the highway. Leaving Miami is something I never thought I would be able to do, but the thought of it was comforting. I finally get to go back home. Well, what passed for a home since my family is not my family. I look in my bag and pull out the photos of my mom and dad. "What's happening to me?" I ask as I stare at the photos. *Maybe, if I do find my parents, they can give me some answers. Lord knows I need them.* I place the photos in my lap and try to relax. It would be a long drive to Charlotte, so I might as well get comfortable. Eventually, I drifted off into a heavy sleep.

As I slept, A man and a woman appear to me in my dream. I cannot see their faces though. They look as though they are towering over me as tall as mountains. A flash goes by, and I see a whimsical land with a beautiful planet in the background. It's nighttime, and everything in sight looks magical. Fireflies hover over almost every square inch of the place. It looks beautiful and yet familiar. The sky is purple and blue with millions of stars dazzling in the night. It disappears and another flash appears, chaos erupts. Creatures are screaming, the moon has turned a horrifying red. Buildings begin to break and crash everywhere, and trees are on fire. It's a giant nightmare. A dark figure stands before me, I cannot make out who the person is, but I can see their eyes. They were a bright, golden yellow and ended up changing to a sinister red. The figure casts spells that spread across the land. I watched as the person slays innocents. It then looks at me, stands before me as nothing other than the epitome of pure evil. It smiles a viciously creepy grin and floats towards me. The figure then strikes at me, and I jump up in sheer terror. My hands are clenched, and I am drenched with sweat. The couple in the next seat look at me nervously. "Are you alright sweetie?" the lady asks me. I sit back down and place my head in my hands on my lap. "Uh, yeah I am fine." I say. *What was that? Who was that?* I think to myself. The lady gets out of her seat and quickly sits next to me. She takes my hand into hers and say, "I see you had a nightmare. I do hope you are okay." I look at her and smile. "Yes, I will be okay. Thank you for being so concerned." She is a dark-hair beauty with smooth cinnamon skin. She looks like she could be a model. She is tall and slender, and she definitely can dress. She is wearing a mid-length black pencil skirt with a yellow blouse. The lady looks to be in her mid-twenties and the man his early thirties. He, however, looks like he is a professor or scientist because he is seriously dressing like a nerd. His brown hair is swooped to the side, and he is wearing a button-down shirt with pins sticking out of the pocket. His pants are also pleaded and looks like he is wearing penny loafers. From the looks of it, he appears to be her husband. The man leans over and says, "It's no problem. My wife and I always try to help others when we can." She nods happily. "Yes, we do." She says. "And seeing that you look very young and are traveling by yourself, it wouldn't hurt to give you a meaningful conversation. I mean we all are going to be on this bus for quite a while so why not get to know each other?" They seem to be very nice people. They were nice enough to check up on me even though they do not know me from a can of paint. I smile in agreement, "I would like that very much." The lady claps her hands in excitement. "Oh yay!" she says. "I'm Judy. Judy

MacEntire and this is my husband-" "Benjamin MacEntire" he cuts in. He waves at me. Judy speaks again, "and we are" she pauses, and they speak in unison, "the tippy tappy toe MacEntire pros!" They finish with jazz hands, and I just stare at them in astonishment. I laugh in amusement. "It's nice to meet you both. I'm Sarah. Sarah Jones." Judy claps her hands. "I love that name for you. It's so fitting, right Ben?" He nods in agreement. Then the bus driver comes on the intercom, "All right folks, we are now pulling off the road to get supplies and gas, so if anyone would like to get some food, or snacks, or just stretch their legs, now is the time to do so." The bus comes to a stop, and we all see that we are surrounded by restaurants and a gas station. I get off the bus so I can grab some food. I walk in and think, *Maybe I should use the rest room before ordering.* I make my way to the back when I see someone out the corner of my eye staring at me. I turn my head and look, but no one is there. I shrug and walk into the lady's room. I use the rest room and walk back out to place my order. I get my food and notice the figure watching me again. I look quickly and see someone in a black hoodie staring at me. I started to get nervous and speed walk my way back to the bus. I get back to my seat and look out the window, making sure the person is gone, but the person is still staring at me. "Creepy much?" I whisper as the bus driver gets on the intercom. I continue to look out the window at the mysterious person as we prepare to drive off. They are still staring at me, and it sends shivers down my spine. I blink and the person disappears from my sight. Where did he go?" I ask myself, nervously. We pull from the parking lot back onto the highway and I breathe a sigh of relief.

Chapter 5

Over the last few hours of the bus ride, I sat in a blur. We were almost at my stop when the image of the stranger popped back into my head. I did my best to try to ignore the strange feeling in the pit of my stomach by talking to Judy and Ben. At some point they got off the bus, having arrived at their destination and I was the last remaining person to get dropped off. By nine AM, we were at my stop. A mixture of joy and fear washed over me as I walked off the bus. I look at my surroundings and relive the memories of being in this town. I clutch onto my belongings and walk the six blocks to Providence Street. Every street I pass, memories of me playing with my friend's flood back into my mind. One minute, I had friends, the next, I was alone. I frown at the thought. Those memories were seriously bittersweet. I shrug the thought off and pick up my pace. Providence Street was just up ahead when I stumbled upon the old mechanic shop my mother's letter mentioned. I clear my throat in anticipation. I look around and it looks like it has been abandoned for years. The only difference is the fact that the gate was wide open instead of locked. I slowly make my way past the gate, trying to see if I recall who used to own the place. It would be surprising if the owner still operated out of this dump but that was a slim chance. There was rust on every corner of the property. Everything that once was good and could be used, is now trash. The door is cracked and broken, the bushes are overgrown as well as the grass, and the building could seriously use a paint job.

The paint was no longer a cream color. Dirt and vines cover the building as well as the rust. I start to doubt coming here and turn around to walk away when the door opens, and an old man appears. He looks to be in his late 80s and he walks with a cane. He apparently works here from the messed-up mechanic shirt he is wearing with the name Billy written on the name tag. "Well, howdy little lady. Can I help you?" I look at him, clearing my throat. "Yes, do you remember"- I go but he interrupts me. "Shh!" he gestures. "Come closer, child." I inch closer, concerned that someone is watching. "We must avoid the trees." He whispers. I look at him, then the trees and back at him. "Why?" I ask. "Because they seem shady." I sit up giving him a dull look. He bursts out laughing like he was a court jester. "Oh, I crack myself up." He wipes his face and gestures back at me. "I'm sorry sweetie, go ahead." I nod. "Do you remember a couple that came here about sixteen years ago? A Charlene and Roger Jones." I reach into my bag and take out a photo of them for recognition. He looks at the picture and within a split second, his eyes go wide. "Well butter my biscuits and season my greens! You're the little critter that we found." I look at him, "We?" He holds his hand out and gestures to me to come inside.

We walked into his garage and to my surprise, there is barely any tools or cars inside. There is, however, a couch, television, some leftover food, a pillow and blanket. It's as if he lives here. "Do you live here, sir?" I asked him. He shoo's me with his hand saying, "I like feeling comfortable, so I become a couch potato here. I can't be a starch anywhere else." He laughs again. His laugh is infectious, and I start chuckling too. He seems to be a crazy old man but who am I to say. "Now little girl, I knew your parents several million years ago when I was younger." He begins. "It was a dark and strange night, because it was raining and cold. I was closing up the shop and taking out the trash when I heard crying in the alley. Your parents were walking by when I reached the start of the alley and we all saw you, wet and crying. Your mother is the one who picked you up and they took you to the hospital. I never saw you again after that, but I did speak to them, and they said that you were doing good." I smile. "Well after all this time, I just found out that I was adopted." He walked over to the kitchen table and poured a cup of coffee. "Wow. I know that they were nervous about telling you." He says, taking a sip. I frown at his words. "Actually, they passed away six years ago." His eyes went wide at the news. "Oh love, I am sorry to hear that." He takes another sip of his coffee. "But I found out about all of this in this letter." I went into my book bag and pull out the blanket so I could find the letter. As soon as I find the letter, Billy stands to his feet. "Where did you get that blanket?" he asks astonished. I look at the blanket and back at him confused. "Uh, it was the blanket that I was wrapped up in as a baby." He hobbled over and picked it up. He ran his fingers across the crest and looked back up at me. "Do you have any idea what this is?" I shake my head in even more confusion. Before he could say anything, we heard footsteps. In walked two people dressed in black. I couldn't make out who they were until they took off their shades and revealed themselves. "Judy? Ben?" I ask. "Look Ben, we finally found her." Billy jumps in front of me and shoves me back. He takes his cane and pulls it apart, revealing a sword inside. "Stay behind me" he says. "Whoa! What the hell do you think you are doing?" I asked him. He starts walking backwards with me in tow. "They are here to kill you." "No, they're no"- I couldn't even finish my sentence. I looked over at them and they had knives and guns. They both looked at me with creepy looks and started speaking this bizarre language. Billy retaliated by responding in the same language. It was strange because while they talked, I could somewhat understand what they were saying. It was more like I could make out certain words they spoke. It was confusing the whole time. Then without warning, Judy and Ben started to attack. I was terrified because I didn't think we were going to make it. Billy, however, stood strong and ready to defend. *Why would this old man want to defend me? He doesn't have a chance with these two.* I think. On cue, he takes his cane and starts to fight them. I stood there shocked because it was as if he had become a completely different person. He was fast, he was strong, and he could use that sword. As Billy is focused on Ben, Judy takes the opportunity to come towards me. I instantly became frozen. I was too shocked with terror to try to defend myself. I tried to move with all my might, but she came at me like a giant ready to obliterate the enemy. As she slashed the knife at me, I closed my eyes praying I get out of this alive. A strong energy surged within me, and I waited for the pain to emerge, but nothing happened. I waited a breath, and then two. Still, nothing happened. I open my eyes to see that I was not in the same spot as I was before. I somehow ended up further away from her, across the room far. *How did I end up over here?* I ask myself. Judy looks up at me and runs after me. Billy looks over Ben's shoulder and yells, "Kick the table!" I act without thinking and kick the table as instructed. The table moves out the way and the floor opens up. Out comes a shelf with a set of beautiful twin daggers on it. The daggers are nothing like I have seen before. They have the blade in a unique intricate curve that resembles a flame. A thinner blade is nestled on top of the bigger blade with the same design but it curves in the opposite direction. The thinner blade has a sort of writing on it that is beautiful, even if I cannot read it. The handles are what took my breath away. The handles looked like white crystals with a rainbow color shine that draws you in. Around the crystal, was a series of vines that went from the bottom to the top. Something came over me in that moment, like I just knew they were meant for me. I grab them without a second thought and start to think, *how am I supposed to fight her with these? I don't know how to fight.* I look at Billy and he is struggling at this point. I brace myself and try to make my way to him. I strike at Judy, and she retaliates. I begin to dodge her movements and I feel like I am flying. The daggers begin to glow a bright blue out of nowhere and the vines begin to grow. They extend down my forearm and grab hold of me like they were perfectly fitting gloves. Then, the blades retract. Judy takes the opportunity to slash my arm and I stumble backwards. I am about to throw the dagger handles down when the blades reappear. They sliver up the handle and extend longer until it reveals twin swords. I look at them with excitement. "Oh, they are about to get it now."

Chapter 6

I restarted my pursuit to get to Billy, fighting and scuffling about with Judy. She is attacking like a maniac. She slashes left and right and with every movement she makes, I dodge. She finally gets close enough to where she uses her free hand and punches me in the stomach. I wince at the excruciating pain and try to kick her to knock her over. She jumps over my kick and slashes my arm again. At this point, I am beyond pissed. My rage builds within me, and the swords glow again. When my rage is at its peak, the swords retract and reshape themselves to display thick curvy blades that curve from my wrists to my elbows. *These swords are awesome!* I think to myself. "Those are some interesting weapons you have." Judy utters out of breath. "Too bad you won't live to see them. And then, they will be mine." Judy reshapes herself until she looks just like a three-eyed white dragon. I shiver as I watch her change from a human to a monster. As soon as her transformation is complete, she stomps towards me, ready to start again. I don't hesitate and I tuck and roll until I am at her mid-section and manage to slice her stomach with both blades. She roars at the pain and tries to kick me. I dodge and roll again, placing myself behind her. I then slash her legs. She roars again. She becomes enraged so much that she throws a table at me. I roll once more and reach her other side and kick her so hard, that she flies into the wall. I take that moment to run to Billy and stab Ben in the back. He hollers in pain and turns to me. His face then transforms from a human face to something of a reptile. He looked like a white snake or a white gecko with his scales going further and further down his back until he was completely transformed. I jump at the site of him and use the other sword to cut his head off. His body drops to the floor, and I watch as his head rolls a short distance away from us. "Billy are you okay?" I asked him, panting. He stumbles and finds his footing before saying, "I'm fine little one, but you must leave. You need to return."- He takes the sword out of Ben and hands it to me. I look at him confused. "Where do you mean return? Return where?" I ask. Movement in the corner stops us from talking. We look over to see Judy beginning to rise from the rubble and she freezes to see Ben in two pieces. Billy looks back at me and hands me a small circular object. "There is no time, child. You must go!" Judy screams in a rage and races towards me. Billy runs towards her and begins to fight her off. In the midst of the battle, he yells, "Press the button and you will be sent far away from here. Tell them Myantu protected you." Everything he is saying does not make any sense. "I'm not leaving you behind." I yelled to him. He punches Judy and yells, "Yes you are, now go! You must be protected." My heart aches at the thought of leaving him but I listen. I grab my bag by the table and as instructed, I press the button. I am thrusted forward, floating, and nothing but multicolored lights surrounding me. Those lights fly by me fast as lightning and then change to stars and space with swirls of purple and blue blending in. The entire sight looks beautiful. I had never seen such a sight before, and it makes me want to explore it. In the back of my mind, however, I cannot help but be nervous and scared at the fact that I do not know where I am going, and Billy could possibly be dead after I left him like that. *Why would he go to such great lengths to protect me? He doesn't know me. But I am grateful to him because he did save my life.* My thoughts are interrupted when it looks like I am approaching a star. This star is humongous, and the light is extremely bright yet comforting. I close my eyes, the light being too much to bear and crash with a loud thud and I am knocked out cold.

I awake to the feeling of rain splashing on my face. I open my eyes and I find myself in mud. I sit up, wincing in pain. "Ouch!" I cry placing my hand on my head. "Lord, where am I?" I ask. I look around and I see nothing but trees and wildlife. The sky though, had millions of stars and it looked beautiful. I grab my bag and stumble to my feet. "Wait where are my swords?" I look around frantically unable to find them. A small light begins to glow in the distance. I walk towards it and discover that it's my swords. What is more interesting is that they are not only glowing, but floating. *Cool*, I think. They float to me and land in my hands. The blades retract, only leaving the crystal handles and vines behind. "I have to keep these safe. They are way too cool to lose." I say lowly. I put them in my bag and tried to find my way out of the woods. As I walk, I see little specks of light floating all around me. They float closer to me, and I see that they are not just little specks, but little fairies. Some green, some blue, some purple. They all see me and try to get me to follow them. I was a bit nervous to do so, but I did anyway. They took me further into the woods and I stopped to see a beautiful waterfall with a river. Nothing but green grass and flowers lay about, and I was enchanted. The waterfall was soothing and in the middle was a clear view of the moon. I see a large boulder facing the waterfall and I am compelled to sit on it, so I do. I sit my bag down and take off my shoes. The feel of the grass feels nice and soft. I climb the boulder and sit Indian style. I look at the waterfall a bit longer and think, *This place is beautiful. I could get used to being here.* Before I could think of anything else, I heard a slight chuckle. I flinch at the laughter. "Who's there?" I asked with a shaky voice. "No need to fear me my child. I will not harm you." The voice says. It's a feminine voice, sweet and soft, but powerful at the same time. "Who are you? Where are you?" I ask. I'm looking around, leaving no area unchecked but I see no one. In front of me, a light flickers and a light blue, misty figure forms. "I am the guardian of this enchanted forest." The mist says. "You are here, in my home. This lake is called the Lake of Truth. Others will call it, the Lake of Whispering Thoughts." I scoot back, feeling a bit nervous about talking to a mist. "W-well, what is your n-name?" I ask. "I am the Deity of Truth, but you can call me Hu'Tilli." I nod my head. "I am"- she interrupts me. "Sarah Jones" I look at her shocked. "How do you know that." I ask. "My ability allows me to know the truth." "Okay, so can you tell me anything about this place?" The spirit shakes her head. "I cannot speak on it at this time. But I can tell you that you are home, and all will be explained to you in the near future." I lower my gaze to my hands, feeling sad. "In the meantime, why don't you go and take a look around?" Hu'Tilli inquires. I pause contemplating whether I should or shouldn't, but I know that staying here in the woods wouldn't be a good idea, so I nod. I grab my things, put my shoes back on and try to find a way out.

I finally make it out of the woods, and before me I see a giant palace. The structure looked strikingly similar to my crystal daggers. It was unique and beautiful. Something in me felt whole and content. I couldn't explain the feeling, I never felt like this before. Before I could take a step towards it, I duck down, seeing creatures walking about. They are dressed alike, so I assumed they were soldiers. They walked pasted me talking amongst each other, but it sounded like they were gargling. I waited until the coast was clear, and I made my way to the beautiful looking garden. I crouch down by these unique flowers. They looked very exotic, and I felt like I could get lost in them if I stayed. But I pressed on. I manage to get pass the garden as I reach the stairs to the back doors. There are double stairways that go up to a balcony and I see that there is no one in site. I crawl my way up the stairs and hide behind a tall plant. I peak around the corner, and no one is around. I creep in the door, and it looks like I am on the second floor, which is very high up. *I need to find a room to hide in. One that isn't occupied.* I slowly make my way to each pillar trying to make sure I am not seen. On the first floor, there weren't many people about, but you could see guards every now and then. Each one looked different. None of them were human. All were a different species of creature. I was amazed and frightened at the same time, but I knew if I didn't find a place to hide, they surely would find me. I stumble across another hallway with a series of doors. *Surely one of these were an empty bedroom.* I think. I checked the first one with double doors, and it was a library. I checked another, and it's a bedroom but looked to be occupied. "Maybe these are the maid's quarters or something." I whisper. I checked several more doors and see that they are all similar. At this point, I am getting very nervous being exposed like this. Being out in the open when you are trying to break in is never a good thing. I turn around and make my way back to the first hallway so I can leave, and I almost make it when a door opens up and slug kind of creature, I suppose is a maid slithers out. She stares at me, and I begin to get nervous. She screeches a loud scream and I take off running. I get to the first hallway and an alarm goes off making me panic. I turn around and see guards running down the hallway and I take a chance and jump over the balcony to the first floor. I land with a loud thud and begin to run away when I run into a huge brick wall. I looked up to find not a brick wall, but one of the soldiers. I don't let that stop me and I try to get away from him. He grabs me and other guards surround me. I am screaming and grunting, trying to break myself free but it is no use. They are too strong, and I am just me. The alarm goes off and the crowd of guard's part ways to show the King walking towards me. He is tall like a mountain, has really dark skin, a chiseled face, and angry eyes. I am already a mess, covered in mud from head to toe, my hair soaking wet and covering my face. He looks at me with rage and I am scared shitless, but I don't show it on my face. I just looked away from him appearing upset. "Who are you?" he asks. His voice is so demanding and strong that I flinch at his words. I am too scared to talk so I remain quiet. He raises my head and asks again, "Who are you?" This time his voice gets louder and booms throughout the room. I still remain quiet. He growls at me and demands, "Take her away! I'll deal with her later." I am lifted up off the floor and carried away when we all hear a soft "Wait." Everyone stops in their tracks and turns to see the Queen.

She stands before us in a white silk night gown. Her hair was long, thick and black with curls that were halfway pinned up. She glides towards me as if she is floating on air. She reaches me as she stands beside her husband. She gives him a sideways glance and looks back at me. She walks closer and looks me in my eyes. I am nervous because she is not saying anything, and I am not sure what she is going to do. She smiles a soft smile and takes my left hand. "Do not be scared." She whispers. I am shaking at this point. She takes a deep breath and stares at me. Her eyes turn a light green and I freeze, mesmerized by them. The light appears on her arm, going all the way down in some kind of weird writing. I hold my breath in anticipation, not knowing what she is going to do. When I think she is about to magically punish me for entering her home, she blinks. The light goes away and she looks at me with concern. She holds my chin up and smiles again. She looks me over one more time before saying, "Take her to one of the guest rooms." I blink. Her husband yells, "What?!" She doesn't even look in his direction. "Be sure she bathes, and has clothes to sleep in." The maid standing next to her nods and walks off. "We will talk more over breakfast, okay? No one is going to harm you. You are safe." Her husband yells out in protest as we all walk away, and I am escorted to a room upstairs. It's faint, but I hear her calming him down. I walk up a different set of stairs in the opposite direction and a cheetah looking maid walks beside me as we reach a long hallway. We soon reach the end and turn a corner to a longer hallway, and she stops at the last door in the center with large double doors. In her accent, she says, "We are here miss." She opens the door and stands aside to allow me in. I walk in and see this giant room that looks like a dream. Beautiful designs on the walls, a unique chandelier that twinkles, a king size canopy bed with cream colored silk sheets, and a balcony that overlooks the garden in the backyard. I am flabbergasted. "If you acquire anything else miss, I will be two doors down." The maid says. "Everything you need to bathe is in the bathroom and your night wear is in this wardrobe." I nod my head, "Thank you." She doesn't even look at me. It dawned on me that she never looked in my direction while talking to me. I extend my hand out, "I'm Sarah." She takes a step back, scared that I am going to do something to her. "Have a nice evening miss." She says as she hurries out of the room. I look around and try to make sense of the fact that I went from being a prisoner to a guest in a palace. While pondering over it, I drop my bag and make my way to the bathroom to take a shower. I take my time in the shower, making sure all the dirt is off of me and my hair. I dry off and get dressed, hoping that no one will try to come in here. I walk out of the bathroom and hop into bed feeling exhausted. The bed is extremely soft, and I immediately drift off to what feels like the most peace I have had in forever.

Chapter 7

I awake to the sun beaming on my face. Looking around, I forgot where I was for a moment. Then it dawned on me that I am in some kind of foreign land with a king and queen. I sit up in bed and see that the maid from last night is standing in the room by the door. "Were you standing there this whole time?" I asked her. She nods her head in response. "The King and Queen request your presence at breakfast miss." "Requests?" I ask folding my arms. She nods again. I roll my eyes. "I will be there in a minute." I say. "Just let me get dressed." I roll out of bed and grab my bag. Walking to the bathroom, I think about what I am going to wear. I reach in and grab my green army pants and a white crop top. I put them on and slick my hair into a messy bun. I don't even bother to put on shoes or socks. I quickly brush my teeth and wash my face then scurry out to meet the maid. We leave the room and slowly walk to the dining room. The maid remained silent as we walked, and I was concerned as to why she was so quiet. I wasn't going to hurt her or anything. "Do you know what time it is?" I asked her. I'm trying to make conversation with her as we walk but she remains silent. Something is definitely a miss, and I am going to get to the bottom of it. We make it to the dining room, and it is humongous. There is artwork surrounding the walls and a mural on the ceiling. They have giant doors that lead outside to the back gardens and on the opposite side, a small tea table for teatime. At the back of the room is another flight of stairs and finally, a crazy long dinner table that could fit at least thirty people. Food covered every inch of the table and the King and Queen sat on opposite ends, already enjoying their meals. The Queen rose when I entered, "Good morning my dear! Thank you for joining us." she says, overjoyed. She extends her hands, and ushers me over to her. I look at the King and he seems displeased with my presence. *Tough shit* I think to myself. I walk towards the Queen, and she gives me the biggest hug ever like she hasn't seen me in years. "Come" she says as she walks me to the center of the table. It really puzzles me that she is being so nice when she doesn't know me. I sit down quietly and watch her as she makes her way back to her seat. As soon as she sits, she picks up her utensils and begins to talk again. "I hope that you slept well." She says. The King huffs at the comment and bites into some kind of fruit. I roll my eyes at his sound effect and nod my head in her direction. "Uh, yeah. I did." I answer. The servants began to fix my plate and I sat there puzzled. None of this food looked natural and I was extremely nervous about eating it. "Oh, don't hesitate to eat as much as you want. Nothing but the best food sits at this table." The Queen says. I sit silently and just nod my head. *I don't trust these people.* I think. *What is any of this food?* "So, what is your name? We never got it last night." The King huffs again and I begin to feel annoyed. *There is no way I am giving him any bit of information. He doesn't deserve it.* I protest in thought. *He is acting like a child though and it is pissing me off.* I look at the Queen and say nothing. She looks at me with concern and tries again. "I'm Queen Marie and this is my husband, King Mathyis." I look at the King and he is staring at me with such disgust. I roll my eyes and pick up my fork to try to eat the food. My hand shakes as I lift it to my mouth. I slowly take a bite and to my surprise, the food tastes awesome. I have no idea what any of this is, but I continue to eat it. I try something different, and it is just as good as the other option. I am halfway through my breakfast when I remember why I am there and need to get home. I put my fork down and say, "When can I go home?" The Queen looks at me. "Well that depends on how you got here my dear." She says. "Yeah" the King finally speaks. "How did you get here?" His tone was sharp and anything friendly. "Mathyis" The Queen scoffs at him. "That's enough" At this point, I have had enough. "Yeah, you are out of line" I snap at him. He stands up and leans on the table. "Watch your tone, human." I stand and lean towards him. "I don't have to do a damn thing." The Queen stands and tries to calm us down. We clearly cannot hear her at this point. "You do not come into my palace, into my kingdom, and speak to me this way." I knock my plate out of the way, and it shatters on the floor. "And you do not turn into a colossal asshole when someone has no idea where they are and clearly needs help. Is this how you treat all of your subjects? With no compassion?" He was livid. He shoots across the table in a flash, his eyes beginning to glow white. We are standing face to face, both looking like we are ready to pulverize each other. "That's enough out of both of you!" the Queen yells. We both look at her, snapping out of our stare down. "Marie she can't just come in here looking like this and we not knowing who she is and"- "That's enough out of you." She interrupts. She is beyond angry with him. I look back at him. "Pathetic" I say and storm off out the door to the back yard. I needed to get some space from him and fast before we were scrapping.

I walked around the garden for a while, feeling more calm now that I was away from him. I am not sure how long I have been out here, but I don't care. As I walk, I feel very content with feeling the grass beneath my feet. I reach the center of the garden and become surrounded by flowers and a fountain. I sit on the ground and lay back, just wanting to feel the breeze and forget everything around me. Without even realizing it, I fall asleep to the sounds of nature. Sleeping soundly, I see a small flame glowing in the distance. "Hello?" I say. I must be dreaming. I am surrounded by nothing but darkness and this small flame. I walk towards the flame, and it starts to call out to me. I stare at it, the flame looks so calming and pretty. I reach for it and as soon as I touch it, I am whizzed to a different area. There is nothing but homes and wildlife around me. It looks beautiful, until it flashes, and I see everything on fire. Once again, I am standing before chaos. People are running and screaming. I watch as a building crashes on to the people around me and tears form in my eyes. A sinister laugh snaps me back and I turn to see the dark figure destroying everything in its path. The figure is forming, and I see that it's a woman. She is floating up high and within a blink of an eye, she is floating in front of me. Her red eyes are piercing my soul. I try to speak but no words come out. I cover my mouth in terror. I don't know what she is going to do to me. She smiles the evilest smile I have ever seen and says, "I. am. THE END." I jumped up scared out of my mind. I am looking around frantically and see that the same maid is crouching in front of me, looking confused. She hands me a small note and it reads:

Please forgive my husband. I would like to speak with you over tea. Would you meet me on the balcony for tea? Just us girls.

-Marie

I look at the maid as she rises, and she extends her hand to help me up. I take it after taking a deep breath and getting myself together. "Follow me, please." She struggles to say. I nod and we begin walking. She once again says nothing as we walk, and I try not to push anything out of her. We reach the palace and walk up the outside stairs to the balcony when the Queen comes into view. She is sitting down, sipping tea, and clearly waiting for me to arrive. She stands as soon as she sees me with a big smile on her face. She gestures to the chair as I get closer. "Please sit." She says nicely. I sit down and fold my arms, not wanting to go another round of anger. "Would you like some tea?" she asks as she sits. I shake my head. "What do you want?" I snapped at her. "I want to again apologize for my husband's outburst." She says. "It was wrong of him to act such a way and I am ashamed that he did." I sat up, realizing that she is being genuine. A small smirk spreads on my face. *Maybe I can talk to her. Maybe she can help me get home.* I think. "Well, what's his problem?" She frowns and holds her head down. "It's no excuse why he acted that way, but he has been this way about all people after a tragedy happened in our past." I look at her, actually concerned. She continues, "We lost our daughter when she was a baby, and he was betrayed by his best friend." My eyes go wide at her comment. "I'm so sorry." I say. She shakes her head. "It's alright. We are getting by the best way we can, but I can say it is different. Things are not the same since she disappeared." I can see tears forming in her eyes and she wipes them away. I didn't want to pry, so I tried to help by changing the subject. "So, what is this place?" She gathers herself and smiles again. "This is Xan'Zuli. A world apart from your world. Here, we have many races and species as our loyal subjects." I pour myself a cup of tea as I listen. "This world is located not too far from your planet Earth." My face expression looks shocked when she says this. "How did you know I was from Earth?" I ask. She chuckles. "Well for one, the way you dress is nothing like here, two, from first sight, I can tell you are human, and three, I am an empath as well as having a gift of knowing." I smile. "Cool" I say before taking a sip of tea. "This is really good by the way." "Thank you" she says. "Do you remember when we met the night before and you saw me using my powers?" I nod my head as I remember it. "Well, that was me using my powers. I saw that you were scared, and you had clearly been hurt before you arrived, so I wanted to make sure you were okay. Which reminds me." She places her hand on my black, swollen cheek and her eyes begin to glow. The glowing symbols trail down her arm and reaches her hand. My cheek begins to feel warm, and I am instantly comforted by the feeling. I close my eyes and inhale a deep breath. After a breath, then two, she removes her hand. "There, that's better." I place my hand on my cheek. It doesn't hurt and it doesn't feel swollen anymore. "What did you do to me?" "I healed you." She says happily. "This is another one of my powers." I smile at her. "Thank you." She nods as she accepts my praise. Taking another sip of my tea, I think, *I just might learn to like this lady.*

Chapter 8

Time goes by as the Queen and I talk about Xan'Zuli history, its culture, and so on. After tea, she walked me around the palace explaining everything. I was actually intrigued by it all. She did ask me a few questions about myself but did not pressure me with the really difficult questions, like how I got so bruised up or my family. I was able to tell her my name and where I am from. After a while, I had to ask her, "So when will I be able to go home your majesty?" She stops walking. "Well again, I need to know how you got here." I nod my head and reach into my pocket pulling out the device that brought me here. I stare at it for a moment, remembering Billy or shall I say Myantu. I give it to her, "It was given to me by a man named Myantu." Her eyes go wide at the name. "Myantu gave you this?" she asks, taking it. "Yes. Wait, you know him?" I asked confused. "Myantu was one of the best craftsmen I have ever seen." She claims. It made sense seeing how the dagger he had were beyond awesome. "We all thought he was dead after the battle all those years ago." "Well, I guess not because he is alive and well." I say. "Well, I hope he is still alive." I mutter. She looks at me with a strange look on my face. "What makes you say that?" she asks. I explained to her the situation on how I got here and then she understood. "Ah" she says. "He is always looking out for people." I smiled at her and nodded. "Well, no worries, we will try to find him and bring him home." she proclaims. "But I do want to let you know that it might be a while before we can send you home." I pause a beat. "Why?" I ask. She looks at the button and back at me with a sad look on her face. "The device that brought you here is very old and no longer is used here in this world. After our daughter disappeared, the man who tried to take her, tried to use it to enter your world and we made sure to destroy everything that had to do with portal jumping. It is our absolute law to never use it." I placed my hand on her shoulder. "That must have been tough for you, not being able to use it yourself to find your baby." She holds her head down and nods. "I know she is still out there. I can feel it. As a mother, you can't help but have hope for such things. I will never give up and I know she will be found." Before I could speak, the door down the hall opens up and the King walks out. He sees us and I instantly get mad at his presence. I look back at the Queen and say, "Well I think I better take off so you two can talk. I will see you later." I walk away before she can even speak. I make it around the corner and exhaled a huge breath, not knowing I was holding it. *I don't know why this man makes my blood boil so much.* I think. *I got to get ahold of myself.* I make my way back to the front of the palace when I stumble across a huge set of double doors. Curiosity gets me and I go to open the door. It opens without a problem, and I see mountains of books. It's a library. My mouth drops to the floor as I walk further inside. "This is incredible." I say aloud. My voice echoes throughout the room. Then the doors open up and the King enters the room. I roll my eyes. "Can I help you with something your majesty? Or are you here to yell at me again?" I snap. He doesn't say anything. He walks up to me, standing next to me with his hands behind his back. "This library has been in my family for thousands of years. Everyone has come here for knowledge about anything and everything. It is one of the greatest places to be in inside the palace." I look at him then turn my head quickly when he realizes I am staring. "It is nice in here." I say lowly, clearing my throat. "I do like to read books." He smiles a small grin. "I am sure you excelled in school." I lower my head, remembering the fact that I am no longer in school. "Yeah, I was." I stretch out. "What do you mean by that?" he asks. I sigh a strong sigh and say, "Before coming here, I was expelled from school for destroying school property and putting a student in the hospital. I am not sure how I was able to do that, but I pushed the table through the cafeteria wall and broke some of her bones." He looks at me astonished. "What? I was tired of being bullied, okay? Sue me!" I fold my arms, not caring that he is still watching me. He chuckles at me. "No need to feel discouraged. You can always learn new things while you are here." I turn and look up at him. "What?" He turns to me. "I know my behavior was not up to par earlier and for that I apologize. I want to make amends by offering you lessons of knowledge. At least until we can send you home." I become overjoyed with excitement. "Oh, thank you your majesty!" I shouted. I run over to a shelf and ponder on what book I want to select first. I found one on the nation's language. I was surprised that I selected this book. It was different that my usual study of science and math. So, I decided to give it a shot. The King walks over to the table as I sit down, and he joins me. I began reading the book and to my surprise, the language doesn't seem that difficult. He never hovered and he was patient with me whenever I struggled. We spend several hours in the library learning the language and the nation's history. Before we knew it, it was dark outside and dinner time. "Good heavens!" the King says aloud. "We have overdone today's lesson." I rub my eyes and nod my head. "We sure did." "We better get to dinner before Marie has our heads." He laughs. I laugh along with him. "Yes, your majesty." He places his hand on my shoulder as I stand. "Please, call me Mathyis. Seeing as you are our guest and we are starting anew, we should get rid of the formality, don't you agree?" I shook my head in agreement. "Sarah" I say extending my hand. He politely shakes it as he smiles. "We better get going." I say. We leave the library and take off to have dinner. Finally, the hostility can seize, and we all can begin anew.

Chapter 9

One week later

After being here in the palace for a little over a week, I have grown accustomed to this life. I spend my mornings with Marie and Mathyis over breakfast, I walk with Marie afterwards just to have girl time, that is if she is not bombarded with politics and other Queenly duties. Moments when the King and Queen are needed, I spend my days reading in the library or around the garden. I have picked up on the language quite well and my lessons about the nation's history, its life here are going superbly if I say so myself, and I like it a lot. The only downside to being here is that I do tend to feel lonely. No one knows that I am here other than those that work in the palace and of course the King and Queen. I do wonder what it is like outside the palace walls. And I do wish I could get back into my old routine of working out. I know I used to do it with my dad when I was younger and since they passed, I had no choice but to stop. Now that I am free from my fake family, I can focus on me. At this moment, I am in the library with Mathyis hard at work studying. I see that it is a little bit past noon, and I am bored. I really want to get out and train so I look up from my book and ask in Zul'ese, "Do you have an area where I could train?" Mathyis looks up from his book. "You said that quite well." He smiles. "And yes, we do. On the west side of the palace there is a place where we train the soldiers and another area where I personally train." I close my book with excitement. "Oh, please can we go? I am in desperate need to get out for a bit." He chuckles at my enthusiasm and nods his head in agreement. I jumped out of my seat. "Give me five minutes to change and I will meet you in the backyard." "Okay then." He says laughing. I dash out of the room and try to make my way to my room as fast as I can. *I seriously need to run faster,* I think to myself and the next thing I know, I am shot up the stairs and down the hall. I screech to a halt when I reach my door. "Whoa!" I say, shocked that it happened again. *At least I didn't run into the door this time.* I make my way into my room and change clothes. Marie was nice enough to get someone to make me some clothes. Wearing the native attire feels awesome. I choose to wear the customary native training clothes which consists of brown shorts, a brown crop top, beads that form the waste, and straps that wrap around my arm with the nation's feather attached to it. I look like a Native American with this on, but I rock this outfit. I tie my hair in a low ponytail and make my way to the back yard. I get there with ease and Marie and Mathyis are waiting for me. "Hi Marie!" I say as I approach them. She turns to me and is stunning, wearing a white and gold dress. She looks like a Greek goddess. Her hair is in curls and is partly pinned up. She smiles and reaches out to hug me. "I hear that you two will be sparring today." I nod my head and switch to Zul'ese. "I am so excited about doing it." She smiles and switches languages as well, "Your Zul'ese has come along tremendously. You sound like a native." "Thank you" I say. We all begin to walk outside, and I see a horse and carriage waiting for us. The horse is huge with four eyes, no ears, and six legs. The carriage, however, is a beautiful white and gold opened carriage with a gorgeous pattern. We climb in and set the course to the training grounds. Looking around, I see that the palace yard is tremendously large. "I never knew how big the grounds were." Marie looks out into the fields,

"Yes, it's been like this for generations. I fell in love with it when I first moved here." "Yes, she was very excited about these grounds, so every day I took her around. Always some place new, so she could explore." Mathyis says. Seeing them together brings me much joy. They really appear to be in love after all of these years. *I wonder how old they really are.* I think. We rode along and talk for another ten minutes before we arrive at the training area. We get off and Marie takes her seat on her shaded throne while Mathyis and I prepare ourselves to spar. There are other soldiers around, but they are standing guard to protect us from harm. "Are you ready, Sarah?" Mathyis asks. I finish my stretches and nod. "I am" "Then let us begin." He smirks. We get into our positions, and I throw the first punch. I miss. "Never be too eager to attack your opponent." Mathyis says. I tried again and he clipped me. I fell to the floor with a loud thud. "Do not leave yourself open." I flip myself up and begin pulling a series of kung fu moves that I learned. Every single strike I make, he dodges. I began to get angry. *This has never happened to me before. I was always very good at kung fu and yet, I feel like an amateur.* It goes on like this for a while and I can't take it anymore. I walk over to the edge of the ring and grab my small bag that I remembered to bring with me. I pull out one of my crystals and it immediately forms into a sword. Mathyis and Marie go silent as they watch me form another stance. "Where did you get those?" he asks, shocked. "Fight now, questions later." I say. I begin to swing the blade and like before, I miss. My rage starts to grow as I continue to miss. Mathyis seems distracted, so to end it he makes a quick move that I have never seen before to put me on my behind. I couldn't take it anymore.

My anger is at its peak and I begin to feel the same powerful energy I felt back on Earth. I stand back up and close my eyes. I take deep breaths trying to calm my mind. After the fifth breath, I didn't feel like myself. I felt different. I opened my eyes and as if my body had a mind of its own, I lunge forward and within a blink of an eye, I am moving fast. Mathyis sees the change in me and retaliates by using his powerful strength. My swords begin to glow bright, and I manage to knick him in the shoulder. He grabs hold of my arms trying to stop me, but I try to pry him off. "Sarah, calm down." He yells, but I cannot control myself. I release the swords and try to punch him, but he catches the powerful blow, and the wave sends me flying back. I land on my back, and I am knocked out.

I woke up and I found myself in bed. I feel weak and lightheaded. I try to sit up, but my body rejects the movement. *How did I get in my room?* I think to myself. I try to sit up again and Marie sits down beside me and says, "No no no, stay down. Your body has been through a lot, and you need to rest." "What happened to me?" I strain out. "You had a sparring accident and you have been out for almost four days." She says. My eyes go wide, and I push myself up. "What?! Ouch!" She pushes me back down. "Please stay down or I will have to heal your body again." "Why would you have to do that?" I ask. She takes a deep breath and says, "Your body somehow became unstable when you became unconscious. I had to act fast and heal your body for a full day." She pauses before continuing, looking puzzled. "Did you know you have powers?" I shake my head. "No. I just found out. I honestly don't know what I have." She makes a face but quickly fixes it. "Rest now. All will be better when you heal." I relax and close my eyes, drifting back off to sleep. Sometime later I wake again, feeling more rejuvenated. I am able to sit up and stretch my body. I climb out of bed and make my way to the bathroom to clean myself up and dress. Apparently, I slept the rest of that evening into the new day. I quickly shower and dress in some of my regular clothes, a tank top, and shorts with sneakers. I let my hair down, loving how it looks despite me always struggling with it. I quickly combed through it and made my way downstairs for breakfast. I arrive at a steady pace and Mathyis and Marie are appalled to see me awake. "Sarah!" Marie exclaims. "Good morning, guys" I say in Zul'ese. "It's good to see your awake." Mathyis says pulling out my usual chair. "Yeah, I feel much better. Whatever you did to heal me worked. Thank you." I say to Marie. I began to fix my plate and dive in, not realizing how hungry I was. It made sense due to being unconscious for the past few days. As I ate, Mathyis and Marie were being awfully quiet. I look at both of them and they are just watching me as I eat. "Uh, is something wrong?" I ask. "You know it is rude to stare, ya know?" They both adjust themselves, looking nervous to say anything. The tension in the room felt incredibly heavy and whatever elephant was in the room needed to be said. I place my fork down and say, "Okay, what is going on? You both are acting weird, and this is not like y'all." "Sarah, it's not best to speak about this over breakfast." Marie says. "No now is the perfect time." I rebuttal. Marie looks at Mathyis with this weird look on her face like she doesn't know what to say. Mathyis tries next, "Um, Sarah, how old are you?" I look at him, confused by the question. "Uh, I'm sixteen. I just turned sixteen." I say. Marie's fork dropped and they both go wide-eyed. At this point I become nervous. "Seriously guys, what is going on?" I ask. I switched to Zul'ese, "You both are scaring me." Marie sighs and rises. She makes her way over to me and sits next to me. Mathyis does the same and sits on the opposite side. "Sarah, do you remember the story I told you about our daughter disappearing?" I pause to think, trying to recall the story. "Well, the only thing you said was that your daughter disappeared, and a man tried to go after her and you stopped him by destroying your portals." She nods her head and places her hands in mine. "Well sweetie, that's not the full story." I looked from him to her and back again. "Well, what is the full story? And what does this have to do with me?" I ask, my anxiety growing by the second. "Mathyis? Do you want to explain?" Marie asks him. Mathyis looks at me with a sad look on his face. He looks like he is on the verge of tears. "Well, our daughter had just been born when we were under attack. It turns out that the enemy that was attacking us was none other than my best friend, Zurnik. He wanted her powers to take over our world and yours. We tried to protect her as best we could. Marie was still recovering but she risked it by putting the baby down with a protection spell and came to my defense. The floor beneath us began to cave in and that was the moment the baby disappeared. We watched her disappear. We wanted to go find her, but we didn't want to risk him finding her, and with the protection spell in place, it would be hard to detect her. So, we made the most difficult decision of our lives, to destroy all portal devices, and hope that she would be safe until we could find her." He paused and inhaled. "That was sixteen years ago." I pondered over everything he said, and it dawned on me what he was insinuating. "Your saying. That I"- "Your our daughter, Xanyic."

Chapter 10

My entire world has shattered. I am falling into a sea of emotions after hearing the words, "Your our daughter, Xanyic." *I'm their daughter? I'm a princess?* A million questions formed in my head. All of it was hard to process. As much as I wanted to speak, I couldn't form the words. I was so choked up that all I could do was breathe. "Sarah, please say something." Marie says. I stand on my feet, not even bothered by the thud of the chair falling over. They both stand and continue to stare at me. You can see across their faces that they are holding their breath, waiting for me to say something, but I am so far gone, I have nothing to say. "I need time to think about this." Without another word, I walk away. I can feel their eyes on me as I leave the room, but I am too bothered by this to turn around. I make my way to my room, trying to contain my tears as they start to fill up my eyes. I make it to my room in a rush and close the door. Finally, alone, I sank onto the floor, and I began to cry. One part of me is happy at the fact that I found my birth parents, especially after going through all that other bullshit just to get out. The other part of me was frustrated and sad. *How could I be a princess? I'm a nobody and no one cares about me*, I think. I sit and really wonder why they didn't look for me. If they did, why didn't they look harder? I couldn't think straight. *Am I supposed to really believe that they are my parents? What am I going to do? How can I really know what is true and what is a lie?* I couldn't take it anymore. I stand on my feet and walk over to my bag that was left on the chair in the corner. I pull out my iPod and turn to the first song that I see. 'The Final Episode' by Asking Alexandria pops up and begins booming in my ears. I grab one of my couch cushions and make my way to the balcony. The balcony is beautiful, overlooking the garden and the Enchanted Forest where I first arrived. I look above the balcony and see a small roof that covers part of the balcony and wonder, "If I really do have powers, I should be able to jump onto this roof." I tried it out by doing a little hop and I went further then what I expected. I smile at the thought of having powers and jump higher, making it to the roof with one hand. Now I am dangling from the roof, trying to figure out how to pull myself up. "Lord please don't let me buss my ass on this balcony." I say. I take the cushion and toss it up, now holding on to the roof with both hands. I pulled myself up slowly, relieved that I made it in one piece. I set myself up on the edge and laid back. I am surrounded by beautiful pink flowers and vines that smell fantastic. I close my eyes, inhale their scent, and try to get lost in the music. I drifted off to sleep, not caring that the booming music was still in my ears. I wake a short time later, feeling a slight chill in the air. I sit up and realize that it's nighttime. "Have I been asleep that long?" I ask myself. I take the ear plugs out of my ears and see that my iPod is now dead. The wind blows again, and I shiver at the coldness. I slide off the roof back onto the balcony and make my way inside my bedroom. The door opens and a maid walks in, carrying a tray of food. "Your highness," she says in Zul'ese. "Please do not call me that." I say back. She bows her head in shame. "My apologies miss. I just wanted to bring you your dinner. King's orders." She sits the tray down on the coffee table by the couches and walks out of the room. I walk over to it and see the food at a lid on it along with a note.

Xanyic,

I tried my best, but I believe this is your favorite food, according to Marie. I hope you enjoy it.

Love,

Dad

You gotta be kidding me? I think. *Did he really just call me Xanyic? Did he really just call himself dad?* I was livid. *How dare he say such things? My name is Sarah, and I had a dad.* He had no right! I begin pacing the room back and forth, too frustrated to think straight. I couldn't live like this. I couldn't be here anymore. I needed to get out of here and get back to Earth. It is clear that I have overstayed my welcome and it's time to go. I grab my bag and put all of my things inside it. I walk out of the room and see a set of guards walking down the hall. "You!" I say in Zul'ese. *Let's hope I can speak to them fluently.* I think. They jolt at attention and bow as I approach. One of the guards that looked like a fish said, "Yes princess? How may we be of service?" I eyed them both and said, "Please don't call me that. Where is the King and Queen?" They both looked at each other at my comment. The second guard, who clearly was frog said, "Right this way your highness." I roll my eyes, "It's Sarah," I snap. They escort me to Mathyis and Marie, who are once again in the dining room having their dinner. They stand when I walk in the door. "Darling! You're here," Marie says. I stand by the door, looking back and forth between both of them. I stopped on Mathyis, and he looked at me with concern. "Xanyic what is wrong?" he asks. My blood boils at the question. "My name is Sarah," I growl. I clench my fist, trying to control my anger, but I can't help it. Mathyis puts his hands on his hips and says, "Your name is Xanyic. Honey, talk to us. As your parents, we want to be able to help and understand." My anger rises and I feel that amazing energy surging through me again. "My name is Sarah," I snap. My eyes begin to flash between gold and brown. "Do not use that tone with me, young lady. As your father"- I lost it then. "YOU ARE NOT MY FATHER!!!" I yell. I jump and lunge towards him, knocking him across the table onto the floor. We slide from the table to the steps leading to the back door and I begin to beat him. He tries to pull me off of him, but I am too strong. I punched him in the stomach. I punched him in the face. Tears fill up my eyes and pour down my face. I am so angry and sad, but I cannot stop. I keep punching his face, left and right, "You don't know me. You don't know me. YOU DON'T KNOW ME!!!!" I yelled at him. I continue punching him, ignoring the blood that is staining my fist and clothes. The door to the dining room opens and a host of guard's rush in, prepared to stop me. "Sarah stop!" Marie yells in tears. "Nobody move!" Mathyis yells in between my punches. I pause at his powerful command. He stares at me, not fighting back, not looking angry, but with understanding. My body becomes weak as my power decimates. I rise as he continues to stare at me. Marie walks over and touches my shoulder. I couldn't deal with the physical touch, so I took off running out the back door. I ran past all the guards, and they followed, trying to make sure that I was safe. I make my way to the Enchanted Forest, and they freeze, seemingly scared to enter. I don't focus on it; I just keep running. I ran so far that I realized I am lost. I see an opening that has a field and a broken tree stump and make my way towards it. I sit on the stump with my hands covering my face and I cry even harder. I sat there a while unable to control my tears. "I am so lost and confused," I say with more tears. "I can help you," a voice behind me says. I turn to look but get knocked out cold.

Chapter 11

I awoke to the sound of a hammer banging. I look at my surroundings and see that I am in some kind of cave. Nothing but walls of rock and science equipment are scattered everywhere. I see that I am strapped to a table, and I cannot move. I look over and see a man, hard at work with something. He is mumbling to himself and twitching his head to the side. Watching him doing that creeped me out. "Ah, so your awake?" a feminine voice eerily says. I turned the other way to see my maid crouched down looking at me. "You?" I say. "What the hell lady?" She sits up and rolls her eyes at me. The mad man turns around and you can see his snake-like face burnt on the side. He had wild and thinning hair, and an incredibly terrifying psychotic expression on his face. He sees that I am awake and claps his hands with excitement. "She. Is. Awake." He says twitching with every word. He walks towards me, still twitching and hungry for revenge. You can tell by his eyes that he is out for blood. "Your Highness." He says bowing to me. "It is an honor to be in your presence. I am Zurnik." "Lord Zurnik, actually." The maid says. "And I am Annola, soon to be Queen of Xan'Zuli." "Quiet woman!" Zurnik yells. She kneels before him and apologizes. "Why the fuck do y'all have me tied up?" I yell. "Because my dear I want your powers. I want to destroy everything your father holds dear." He says looking at me like he is ready to slice my throat. "And I'm going to do that by making you destroy his world. Then I'll destroy your world with your powers. The universe will be mine." "Why would you want to do such a terrible thing? What did Mathyis ever do to you to be this way?" "He stole everything from me. The love of my life, power, my life, MY FACE!" he growls pointing to his face. "I was in love with your mother, until he came along, and she saw nothing but him." I roll my eyes at him. "So, all of this is because of a woman? Dude you gotta be desperate or something to go through all of this." I say. "I…am…not…desperate!" He yells. "I was a brilliant scientist when I was younger. This is how I met your father. He broke Xanzulian rule and came to Earth knowing that it was forbidden. He met me at my lab. We became friends over time. He believed in me and my work, so he brought me back with him. I eventually met your mother. She was impressed with my work, and she hung around more often. Until, that wretched Mathyis showed his face. From that point on, she was all about him." "Oh, how I wish I could shed a tear for you. But being salty over a girl doesn't mean destroy the world, dumbass!" I snap. He walks over to his desk and pulls out a syringe. "What the hell is that?" I ask. "With this formula mixed with pure Xanzulian blood and the blood of the deities I will be able to control you and you will do my bidding." He says giving me a creepy grin. "Like hell I will!" I yell. I tried to free myself, but I was too weak to wiggle myself free. He injects the syringe into me and a painful feeling in my chest starts to form. I begin to shake, unable to control anything. Zurnik leans down and places his hand on my head. "Now, I am going to leave you here until you are ready for me to perform the forbidden possession spell on you. Soon we will visit your father."

Mathyis stirs as the doctor looks at his wounds. "Your majesty needs plenty of rest. Let's be glad, the princess did not break any bones," the doctor says. "I thank you doctor; I will do that." Marie walks over from the door and sits by his side. "How are you honey? She got you pretty good," Marie asks. Mathyis looks at Marie and grabs her hand. "I am fine, but I am worried about Xanyic. I should be ashamed of myself for pushing her so far. I was so happy we got our little girl back that I wasn't thinking clearly." Marie shakes her head. "My love, we both were happy about having her back after all these years. Anyone would be. She may be upset and confused right now, but she will come around." Mathyis sighs and looks around. I should lay down for a bit. Will you summon me when she returns? We all need to sit down and talk." Marie nods her head. "Sure honey. Rest well, okay?" Mathyis kisses her gently and stands. With guards in tow, Mathyis walks away and out of the room. Marie looked around and noticed that it was getting late, and Sarah hadn't returned to the palace yet. She called a guard over and said, "The princess went out back earlier and has not returned. See that she is alright and protected." He stood at attention and nodded his head in agreement. He walked off without a word and she sat back down, pondering if Sarah was okay.

I wake to find myself still strapped down on the table. "This psycho kept me here all night." I say. "Hello! Get me out of this thing!" Zurnik walks over sipping his coffee and stares at me. "Good morning your highness. I hope you rested well and are ready for another dosage of my serum." I try to free myself from the restraints, but I don't even move an inch. "Dude, seriously, let me go." I say. He shakes his head and places his cup on the counter. "No can do. I will have my revenge. Tonight, during the blood moon, I will have it." *Blood moon?* I think to myself. "You will see," he says as he grabs the syringe on the counter. He injects it into me without hesitation and I begin to feel hazed and woozy. "What are you doing to me?" I mumble. I slip off into a deep sleep when he injects another into me. As I sleep, I feel the presence of evil within me. The feeling builds and builds, and I feel myself slipping into the unknown. My eyes open and I am shaking all over. I notice that my clothes have changed, and I am wearing some kind of black leather bralette with a huge black and red stone necklace with black beading around it and black leather pants. I also have matching stone bracelets and black shoes. My restraints are off me, and I begin to float in the air. I look over and see Zurnik chanting some kind of spell from a book. Swirls of red and black flames circle around me. Above me, there is a skylight. It is nighttime and I see the blood moon beginning to rise. I start shaking faster, unable to speak. My eyes start to roll in the back of my head. My arms are now turning a blueish-black color and red streaks of lightning are forming around it. The red energy is now spreading along with the change of color. I shrieked loudly, unable to take the pain. I squeeze my eyes shut as the pain rises and then, it just stops. "Yes! Yes!" Zurnik yells with excitement. "It has worked! She has turned! Revenge is mine!" I float down and land on my feet. Zurnik walks over to me and looks me over. He sees that my eyes are changing from gold to blood red, and he smiles. "Xanyic?" he asks. "I...am...THE END." I say smiling like the epitome of true evil. "Great! She has changed successfully. Can we go now?" Annola asks, annoyed. "And why are you so attentive to her? I am your queen." He walks up to her and slaps her across the face. "Watch your tone! She is a vital part of us getting what we want so I must be vigilant." She lowers her head and nods. "Hold your head up," he says. "A Queen never bows." She smiles and kisses his cheek. "You're so good to me." He returns the smile and focuses back on me. "Now that you both are done being gross, shall we proceed?" I ask. My voice no longer sounds like mine. It sounds like multiple eerie voices speaking at once. My body doesn't feel like mine. It is as if I am a visitor in my own body. Zurnik walks back up to me and grabs my shoulders. "I want you to destroy the palace and kill Mathyis. Then we can go about taking over Earth, then the universe." My red lightning flashes quickly at the thought of my mission. "Consider it done, Lord Zurnik." I say with a wicked grin.

Chapter 12

Back at the palace in the dining room, Mathyis paces back and forth frantically, worried about his beloved daughter. "Where on earth could she be Marie?" he asks his wife. "I do not know dear but pacing like this will not help. I am worried about her too," she says. "It's been a full twenty-four hours Marie. I cannot help but feel like this is all my fault. If I didn't push her like I did."- "Stop it." Marie interrupts. "Beating yourself up is not going to help. We have search parties out looking for her, she couldn't have gotten far. She is not from here and I am sure someone will notice her seeing that she looks human." Mathyis sits next to Marie and places his head on her shoulders. "I hope you are right honey." The lights begin to flicker, slow at first, then quickly. Mathyis feels uncertain about the lights and begins to draw his sword when the side of the dining room wall explodes in. Mathyis shields Marie from the explosion and the rubble. When it clears, they look up to see Sarah, Zurnik, and Annola walking in. "Xanyic? Honey what are you doing with this man?" Marie asks, worried. I say nothing. Mathyis is very angry at the sight of Zurnik. "What the hell are you doing with my daughter, Zurnik?!" Zurnik laughs at him. "Hello to you to old friend. It's been a long time since I saw you last. Marie? You look as beautiful as ever." Marie grabs hold of Mathyis's arm in a panic. "Mathyis, look at her. She doesn't look like herself." I smiled a malicious scowl at her words. "Sarah, look at me. We are here for you, but you need to get away from him." Mathyis says as he extends his hand to me. I slowly cock my head to the side and say in Zul'ese, "Why would I move from my Lord? He has freed me and now… you all will pay for causing him pain." My eyes turn black as I begin to rise and fly over everyone. I extend my arms and conjure an obscene amount of magical power. Balls of fire grow bigger and bigger within my hands, and I blast them towards the palace walls. "Xanyic, stop it!" Mathyis yells. "She cannot hear you, Mathyis. Her mind belongs to me, and she will do my bidding." Zurnik yells. Mathyis runs to Zurnik and runs into a cloak. "Oh, did you think I wouldn't protect myself this time? He mocks. "Your reign over this world is over and it will be I who liberates the people of Xan'Zuli. I will rule them the correct way and you will watch and suffer knowing that you failed your people. A human bested you." Zurnik laughs as he and Annola walk out of the palace. I follow them out leaving Marie and Mathyis to their sadness and suffering. I make my way to the city, blasting everything in my path. I fly above the town to get a better view and continue to blast left and right. I laughed a menacing laugh. "Die! Die! Die!" I say as I destroy one area to the next. Marie sees me and flies to me. "Sarah! Honey, please stop this. We know you are upset but destroying your home in the name of this evil man is not you," she says pleadingly. I laugh at her words. "I'm not Sarah, your majesty. Sarah is gone, Xanyic is gone. Your precious daughter is no more. I am Mara, Goddess of Death." Marie gasps at Mara. "What have you done to my daughter you feen!?" Marie snaps as she grabs Mara by the arms. Mara chuckles, "I took possession of her body." I grab Marie by her throat and hover her above me. "This world will cease to exist when I am done with it. Now, be gone!" I throw her far in the distance until she is no longer in view. I continue my pursuit of destroying the town. People are screaming and crying but I do not seem to care. I laugh at them and rejoice to see the town crumble beneath my power. "You all will cower before Lord Zurnik," I yell to the people.

Marie crashes to the ground with a loud and painful thud. Mathyis finds her and races to her side. "Marie! What happened?" he asks. Marie coughs and winces at the pain, "She is not our daughter Mathyis. An evil goddess has taken possession of her. We've lost our baby again!" Marie cries, unable to contain her sadness any longer. Mathyis pulls her in close to him, "Not if I can help it." He picks her up and carries her to the palace. Soldiers and servants are scattering left and right trying to get in their positions and help where it is needed. Mathyis yells, "The Queen is injured! Someone come tend to her needs." The royal physician runs over and takes the queen into his arms. "I will care for her your majesty. You needn't worry," he says confidently. "Good." Mathyis says. He bends down to kiss Marie. "Bring our baby home," she says lowly. Mathyis nods then stands. "Believe me, I will," he says walking away.

Zurnik stands at the edge of his cave and laughs hysterically as he watches the city of Xan'Zuli burns to the ground. "Annola! Come and baskin in the glory of this hell!" he yells. Annola walks to his side and watches as the flames of the city glow brighter and brighter. "We are on our way to the top my love," she says lovingly. He looks at her and smiles happily, "Aren't we?" He kisses her passionately until he hears a pebble roll in the distance. He freezes and says, "What was that?" Annola takes a step back and looks around. Mathyis jumps out from the shadows charging in and rams Zurnik into the ground. "You bastard!" he yells as they roll down further into the cave. Mathyis starts to pound his fist into Zurnik's face, not caring about his surroundings. "My daughter Zurnik?! My daughter?! Of all the things in the world, you had to corrupt my daughter?!" Zurnik kicks Mathyis off him and rises to his feet. "This is payback," he says taking a deep breath. "For what? What could I have done so badly to make you despise me so? I met you when you were at a low point in life. People picked on you and your passion for science. I understood it, brought you to my home, knowing it was forbidden for us to be communicating. I believed in you, and you just go and betray me?" Zurnik wipes blood from his lip. "Payback for stealing the one thing I wanted. Because of you, I couldn't be truly happy." Mathyis looks at him confused. "What did I take from you?" he asks. "MARIE!!!" Zurnik yells. "She saw me first when I first arrived and was interested in my work. Only after she sees you, she ends up forgetting about me." Annola walks up to Zurnik. "But you have me now my lord." She says. Zurnik pushes her out of the way. "Stop it! Just stop woman. This is not about you. This is about my revenge. Know your place!" Annola slaps him hard across the face. "I am sick of you talking to me this way. That woman is in the past. Let it go!" "I will never let it go!," he yells at her. "If I have to be second then I am gone. I am supposed to be your number one," Annola snaps. Zurnik rolls his eyes. "I don't need you. I have all the power now." Zurnik does a loud whistle and I instantly hear it. In a flash, I go from the city to the cave and grab hold of Mathyis and Annola's neck. "Mara, be a dear and finish these two off," Zurnik says as he walks off. "With pleasure," I say. I look at Annola, not even caring that she is there, I toss her across the room, and she crashes into the wall and falls to the floor unconscious. "Sarah," Mathyis strains to say. "Don't let them win. You're stronger inside then they will ever be. Your family loves you and we are sorry." Mara laughs ominously. "She's no longer here." I conjured a dagger into my hand and stabbed Mathyis in the stomach. He yells out in pain, and I stab him again. His shrieks causes me to smile, and I toss him outside the cave. He rolls to the edge and falls down the mountain. I watched as he tried to stop himself from falling further but I whispered an enchantment to cause him to miss everything in his reach. He lands to the bottom with a loud thud. I extend my hand and cast a gravity spell. Mathyis then lays flat on his back, grunting and unable to stand. I watch as he sinks deeper and deeper into the ground. "I guess it's time for me to end this," I say aloud to myself. Catching up to Mathyis at the bottom of the hill, I say to him, "You know what?" I magically raise him up in mid air, not allowing him to move. "Your daughter was very easy to take possession of. And now that I have her power, I am going to enjoy watching you die and knowing that the only face you are going to see, is hers." Mathyis closes his eyes as I laugh at his downfall. He sheds a final tear, knowing that this is the end.

Chapter 13

As I am sitting in this dark ominous void, I watch as Mara takes control of me and destroys everything that I have come to love. "Let me out of here! Do not hurt my family!" I yelled to her. But it is hopeless. I am trapped within myself and can only watch as everything comes to an end. Buildings are being destroyed, people are suffering, and there is nothing I can do about it. Worst of all, she is trying to kill my family. I curl into a ball and begin to cry my eyes out. "Why is this happening to me?" I ask myself. "I just wanted to find my real family and feel whole again. Why should an innocent person have to suffer so much trauma? I haven't done anything to anyone. I just wanted to feel loved again. Is that too much to ask?" I cry even harder. "I should have never left Florida. I should have just asked to move in with one of my friends, then I wouldn't be in this mess." "Surely you do not mean that Sarah." A voice says to me. I look above me and see a small light slowly floating down to me. "What is going on?" I ask wiping my tears. "No need to be scared little one," the light says to me, stopping in front of me. The light then changes and appears a woman. She is wearing traditional Xan'Zulian armor, wielding a sword, and wearing a crown. She is smiling at me, and it gives me the feeling of comfort. "Who are you?" I asked her. "I am Famora, the Goddess of Light and the founder of Xan'Zuli. I am also an ancestor of yours." She steps towards me and smiles. "You have to break free from this entrapment Sarah," she says. I lower my head, feeling ashamed of myself. "I cannot escape from here. I don't know how. It's not like I have my powers to get me out and yelling at the top of my lungs won't help." Famora moves closer to me. "Yes, you can. The power is in you." She reaches up and places her thumb on my forehead. "I will give you the power to defeat your enemy and save your people. This power will be temporary, so you must defeat them quickly." I nod my head and close my eyes. Famora begins to glow brightly, and her eyes turn white. The same intricate writing that displayed on the Queen's arm appeared on hers. She started speaking Zul'ese and said, "Powers of Light, powers of strength, all ancients rise. I bestow the powers of the divine, I grant her mine. Release the power, give her the power." Immediately, I felt her power. Lots of lights swirl around me and enter my chest. Her power is strong and mighty, almost intimidating. I begin to glow brightly, and I inhale a deep breath, coming to terms with my new powers. Writing appeared on my arms, glowing a bright gold. I open my eyes and they are glowing also. I part my lips and say, "Time for war."

Meanwhile, Mara still has Mathyis in her clutches. "Are you ready to die?" she asks him. Mathyis appears very weak and faint. He struggles to speak when he says, "You will…rue the day…you messed with…my family." Mara squeezes his throat tighter, trying to break it when she freezes. Her hands start to shake as she struggles to keep him in her hands. "Stop it," she demands. "You will not harm my father anymore, Mara," I make her say. Mara drops him and he lands on his back. "No! This is my body now. You need to just die and give up," she says. "I will never let you win," I say. "Just finish him already!" Zurnik yells in the distance. Mara grabs her head and shakes it frantically. "No!

Stop it!" she yells. She falls to her knees as she continues to fight me. She yells out in pain as I continue to break free. "Give me my body back!" I yell. A humongous light shines on me from my face to my hands. Mara shrieks and it fades away, leaving me behind, finally able to take control of my body again. I crouched down to Mathyis, propping him up on my leg. "Are you okay, father?" I asked him. He coughs and blood shoots out. "I'm fine. You-you called me father," he says. I chuckled at his words. "Well, you are my father, aren't you?" I ask. Before he could respond, the ground began to shake. "You think you can get rid of me that easy?!" a voice yells. The ground opens up and black fog shoots up into the sky. The smoke clears and Mara appears in full form. She is wearing a black lace dress with her long midnight black hair down her back. Her eyes are full of black, and she is furious. "You all will die by my hand," she says. Zurnik appears out of nowhere and starts yelling at Mara. "What are you doing? This is not what we agreed to. You are not doing what you were told to do, and you are ruining everything. Finish the job this"- He instantly gets cut off by Mara. She makes him hover in the air and thrusts him into the side of the mountain and impale him in the stomach with a long metal pole. "You don't get to go around barking orders. You do not run me, I run you," she snaps back at him. She turns to face me and Mathyis. "I'll start with you two," she says low and ominously. "Over my dead body," I say to her. I prop Mathyis on a nearby stump and I rise to my feet. "You will not harm anyone ever again. Not as long as I am here." I say to her. I extend my hands and conjure up my crystal swords. I enhance my power and my eyes glow a golden yellow. My arms and sword follow in a domino effect. My swords then surprise me by forming three small balls of golden fire in between the negative spaces. I take my stance, ready to defend my home. She laughs at me and conjures an army of monsters. "Lets see if you can handle this, princess," she says to me. She points at me, and her army begins their pursuit. I ready myself and say, "Let's dance."

Chapter 14

I race towards the evil army, ready to fight. The first dead monster approaches me, and I slash through him with no problem. I zoom my way further into the crowd and I slash left and right. I am blocking, kicking, and punching each monster that is in my path. Those who meet my blade, disintegrate. I look at my fireballs in-between my blades and I think, "Maybe I can put these to use." I hit a fireball, and it flew across the way, hitting a monster. "Cool," I say to myself. I use my speed and spin around in a circle, extending my blades and shooting fireballs in every direction. A huge portion of the army falls. I look around and still see a good amount of demons left and I wonder, 'How am I supposed to defeat them all? I do not have much time left with these powers." I do not think too much about it and continue to fight. I switch my swords to my arm blades and begin to slash left and right. "Maybe this way I can punch and slash at the same time." I say. Mathyis is looking at me, amazed at my abilities. But he also sees that I am starting to struggle being that there is so many demon soldiers. He takes a whistle that is around his neck. He blows it and a giant spark shoots up in the air, signaling someone. Everyone notices it and I take the opportunity to clear a path so that I can think for a moment. "What am I going to do?" I ask myself. "Maybe I can help," a voice says behind me. I turn and I see the blue mist from the Enchanted Forest. "Hu'Tilli?! What are you doing here?" I asked her. "Hello your highness. I have come to help you in your quest." I look at her, concerned. "How are you going to help me? You are a mist." She laughs at my words. "I have brought help." I look over and see animals of all kinds charging towards the army. I smile seeing that I finally have some help. I look back at her and she begins to change. In the blink of an eye, she goes from a mist to a young girl with wings, and swords. She is wearing a white dress with no shoes. "You're not the only one who can change, your majesty," she says as she starts to run into battle. I stare at her as she starts striking down the monsters, disappearing and reappearing in different areas. Suddenly the ground starts to rumble again. I can hear yelling in the distance. I turn to see my father's army charging into battle and I am amazed at the number of soldiers. Feeling relieved, I put one of my swords up. I look up and I see Mara, who is still floating in the air. "It's time to end this," I say aloud. I conjure up a pair of wings and fly towards her. "Mara!" I yell. "Your destruction ends now." She laughs as she conjures up a sword and swings it in my direction. I swing along with her, and we clash swords together. "You're not strong enough," she says. "I am strong enough to end you," I say. "This entire kingdom will end tonight, and you're gonna watch," she says as she throws a fireball in my direction. I fly back and do a quadruple spin to avoid it. "No, it won't. This is my home; this is my family, and no one is going to take that away from me. I have come to love this place and its people. I will not hesitate to protect them. For the sake of this world and the next, I, Xanyic, Princess of Xan'Zuli and the guardian of Light, will destroy you." I close my eyes and inhale deeply, trying to concentrate on my powers. I begin to glow all over my body, and I center myself before I begin my pursuit. I fly towards her and strike. She counteracts by dodging and striking my arm with a black fireball. The pain sends me flying backwards. I look at my arm and it is bleeding. The pain is excruciating, but I shake it off. She laughs at me and say, "You see? You are too weak to take me on." I fly to her again and slash at her. She flies back and I move quickly by disappearing and reappearing behind her. I stab her in the back with my sword. "I am not weak," I say to her. I shove her forward and blast ice spears at her. She then sends another black fireball. I smack it away with my sword and fly closer to her. I then punched her in the face, and she looked at me astonished. "Yeah, I punched that ass," I say, overly confident. I throw a series of punches and kicks and she struggles to stay upright. Her rage grows and a burst of energy expels from her body. I close my eyes and think, *it's time to end this.* I open my eyes and try to project my power into my sword. My sword glows as brightly as me and streaks of lightning start to flicker from it. Mara looks at me, unphased by my transformation. "It doesn't matter how strong you are, you will never defeat me!" she yells. She raises her hands and a huge dark cloud forms above her head. I can feel her power increasing by the second. Black lightning flickers around her body. She tries to strike me with her lightning, and I dodge it. I race towards her, and she comes towards me. Both of us are completely surged with power. We collide together and our powers crash with a tremendous boom. Everyone stops fighting and looks up at the mixture of light and dark lightning swirling in the sky. When the smoke clears, everyone sees my sword through Mara's chest. Mara looks at me, blood spilling from her lips. "I told you," I say panting. "You will not mess with my family." She falls backward and slowly floats down to the ground. Her body starts to disintegrate and before she reaches the ground, she disappears. Her demon army starts to disintegrate along with her and the crowd cheers. I look for Mathyis and find him next to a guard who is helping him up. I float down to him, relieved he is all right. "You did it" he said. "I am so proud of you." He takes me into his arms and hugs me tight. After everything we have been through, this moment meant everything to me. "Thank you, daddy." I say to him. Mathyis sobs a small cry and releases me. I look around and see that everyone has surrounded us clapping and thanking me. I look in between the crowd and see a translucent Famora clapping along with them. She nods her head and disappears, leaving a final blowed kiss behind. I close my eyes and tilt my head up feeling triumphant and knowing that it is finally over.

Epilogue

I look in the mirror as I finish putting on the final touches to my attire. I am wearing a white and gold cloth dress that exposes my arms and stomach. It looks breathtaking and feels magnificent. I even took the opportunity to straighten my hair and it flows effortlessly down my back. As I finish putting eyeliner on my eyes, a knock sounds at the door and Mathyis walks in. "Are you ready?" he asks me. I look back at the mirror and sigh. "Yes dad, I am ready." He walks over and stands next to me. "You look beautiful," he says. I smile at his words. "Thank you," I say. Another knock sounds at the door and in walks Marie. "Are we ready? It's about that time." She comes closer and stands next to Mathyis. "Oh, Xanyic. You look gorgeous honey. It reminds me of when I first got my powers." I smile at her, and she starts to shed a tear. "Come now my love, let's not shed any tears. We must head downstairs and ready everyone," Mathyis says. She pats her tears away and say, "Your right. We will see you down there, okay?" I nod my head and watch as they walk out of the room. I take another long look in the mirror. "This is it. Time to go," I say. I walked out of the room and four servants holding candles escorted me to the ceremony. We walk a good distance and down a flight of stairs I have never seen before. When reaching the last step, I saw hundreds of candles lit, a few people wearing cloaks and my parents standing before what looked like a small pool. I walk towards the small steps, and I am greeted by an elderly woman. "Glad to see you made it home," she says to me. She removes her hood and I see it is the same elderly lady that helped me at the Handy Mart. "I remember you. You are the lady that helped me back on Earth." She chuckles. "Well, I had to help you get here somehow without completely interfering." I smile at her. "And call me Zula," she says. "Now princess, you have come here to unlock your powers and take your place as the Guardian of Light. Are you ready?" I nod my head and answer, "Yes I am." Another member walks over, carrying a bowl of white liquid. She dips two fingers in it and begins to mark my body. First my forehead, then my arms and hands, next my stomach, and lastly, my legs. I am then led up the stairs to the pool and is instructed to step in and sit on my knees. I step in and the liquid is shallow. It only goes up to my ankles. I await further instructions and I watch the cloaked members form a circle around me. They start chanting in Zul'ese, "Grant her power. Powers, come." The gold liquid then slowly flows up my body and starts encasing me in it. I take a deep breath as it reaches my face and covers me entirely. The liquid then hardens around me and the members blast energy beams at me. They chant louder as the ground begins to shake. The casing begins to crack and beams of light shine through. It shatters to the ground, and I inhale deeply. I open my eyes, and they are finally their true color, gold. "Xanyic?" Marie calls out. "Honey, how do you feel?" I look at my parents, smile and say, "Whole." Zula walks over and stands before me, holding a crown above my head. "Xanyic, daughter of Xan'Zuli, you have now been awakened as the leader of the Guardian of Light. Your duty as leader is to protect all walks of life in our world and the next. With your courage and strength, you will be everyone's hope. With your kindness and compassion, you will bring peace to our nation. Do you accept your new duty? I smile and say, "I do." She walks closer and places the crown on my head. "Let it be known that on this night, we have not only a princess, but a champion. The prophecy has been fulfilled. Praise the heaven and may good blessings be with you always. I rise up and hug my parents. "Well done sweetie," mom says. "We are proud of you," dad says. I squeeze them tighter and think, *Finally, I am home.*

The End

Made in the USA
Columbia, SC
18 January 2025

abefa08c-c448-4169-a0b6-72c4d37babc1R02